LEWIS NORDAN'S

THE ALL-GIRL FOOTBALL TEAM

"The world that Lewis Nordan depicts has not fallen from grace; it has instead collapsed under the weight of it. His stories are, in the words of one of his characters, 'dirty miracles.' An amazing and terribly fine book."
— Fred Chappell, author of
I Am One of You Forever

"Bizarre exploits achieve mythic importance...A collection to savor and treasure." —*Publishers Weekly*

"Nordan has an uncanny eye for humanity's better moments, and an ability to see the potential for nobility even in the most discomfiting situation. Most of these fine stories leave a feeling of wry optimism, a belief that lives can be saved from ruin by sheer assertion of character. Nordan is a powerful writer and an affectionate one; his stories give us an appreciation of the delicate balance between grotesquerie and grace." —*Raleigh News & Observer*

ALSO BY LEWIS NORDAN
Welcome to the Arrow-Catcher Fair

THE ALL-GIRL FOOTBALL TEAM

THE
ALL-GIRL
FOOTBALL
TEAM

Stories by
Lewis Nordan

VINTAGE CONTEMPORARIES
VINTAGE BOOKS
A DIVISION OF RANDOM HOUSE
NEW YORK

FIRST VINTAGE CONTEMPORARIES EDITION, FEBRUARY 1989

Some of the stories herein originally appeared in
Greensboro Review, Harper's Magazine,
Playgirl, and *Southern Review.*

Library of Congress Cataloging-in-Publication Data
Nordan, Lewis.
    The all-girl football team.
    (Vintage contemporaries)
    Contents: Sugar among the chickens—The talker at the
freak-show—Sugar, the eunuchs, and Big G.B.—[etc.]
    I. Title.
[PS3564.O55A8   1989]   813'.54   88-40019
ISBN 0-394-75701-7 (pbk.)

Author photo copyright © 1989 by Ed Sumrok

Manufactured in the United States of America
        10 9 8 7 6 5 4 3 2 1

For Eric
And in memory of Rusty

Attempting to return to the path I came to the fork and went both ways it has not made any difference
—John Stoss

CONTENTS

THE ALL-GIRL FOOTBALL TEAM

SUGAR AMONG
THE CHICKENS

I had been fishing for an hour and still hadn't caught anything. I was fishing for chickens. Mama wouldn't let me walk to the town pond by myself. What else was I going to fish for?

I looked back over my shoulder through the torn-out screened door and tried to see Mama in there. I said, "Mama." I was using the voice that says you're being real good and not fishing for chickens.

Mama said, "You better not be fishing for chickens, Sugar Mecklin, you going to get switched." She's got this ability.

She was out in the kitchen, that was good anyway. I put a fresh kernel on my hook and scattered shelled corn on the slick dirt yard below the porch and dusted off my hands on my white blue jeans. A handful of old hens came bobbing and clucking up to the corn and poked at it with their heads and then raised their heads up and looked around, and then started poking at it again.

I dropped the baited hook in amongst them. I wished I could figure out some way to use a cork. The chickens bobbed and pecked and poked and scratched. I moved my baited hook into the middle of the chickens and eased it down onto the ground and waited. I still didn't get a bite.

My daddy didn't much care whether I fished for chickens or not. My daddy knew I never would catch one, never had, never would. It was my mama who was the problem. She said it would ruin your life if you fished for chickens.

I wasn't studying ruining my life right now. I was thinking about hooking and landing some poultry.

I wasn't using a handline, which is easy to hide if your mama comes up on you. I was using a cane pole and a bream hook, little bitty rascal of a hook. I liked a handline all right, I wasn't complaining. Nothing better for fishing in real tight places, like up under your house on a hot day when the chickens are settled down in the cool dirt and have their neck feathers poked out like a straw hat and a little blue film of an eyelid dropped down over their eyes. A handline is fine for that. A cane pole is better from off your porch, though.

Or I guessed it was. I never had caught a chicken. I had had lots of bites, but I never had landed one, never really even set the hook in one. They're tricky, a chicken.

I really wanted to catch one, too. I wanted the hook to snag in the beak, I wanted to feel the tug on the line. I wanted to haul it in, squawking and heavy and beating its wings and sliding on its back and flopping over to its breast and dragging along and the neck stretched out a foot and a half and the stupid old amazed eyes bright as Beau dollars.

I dreamed about it, asleep and awake. Sometimes I let myself believe the chicken I caught was not just any old chicken but maybe some special one, one of the Plymouth Rocks, some fat heavy bird, a Leghorn, or a blue Andalusian. And sometimes, as long as I was making believe, I thought I might catch an even finer specimen, the finest in the whole chicken yard. I thought I caught the red rooster itself.

The red rooster was a chicken as tall as me. It seemed like it, I swear, when I was ten. It was a chicken, I'm telling you, like no chicken you ever saw before. It could fly. There was no half-assed flying about it. It could fly long distance. Daddy said it could migrate if it had anywhere to go. It couldn't do that, but it could fly fifty times farther than any other chicken you ever saw. This was a chicken that one time killed a stray dog.

I dreamed about that rooster. The best dream was when I caught it not on a handline and not on a cane pole. I dreamed I caught it on a limber fine six-and-a-half-foot Zebco rod and spinning reel, like the ones in the Western Auto store in Arrow Catcher. That's the town I used to live right outside of when I was little, in the Delta. The line on that Zebco spool was almost invisible.

I watched the chickens. There was a fine old Plymouth Rock I would just love to catch. She dusted her feathers and took long steps like a kid wearing his daddy's hip boots. I moved the bait closer to her and held my breath. She started poking around at the corn. She hit the bait once but didn't pick up the hook. My line was taut, so I felt the strike vibrate through the line and down the cane pole to my hands, which I noticed were sweating. I thought, If she hit it once, she just might . . . But she didn't. She stopped eating corn altogether and scratched herself with her foot like a dog.

I tried to listen for my mama. Mama couldn't be expected to stay in the kitchen forever. I needed to say something to her in my I-ain't-fishing-for-chickens voice, but I couldn't. The Plymouth Rock pecked the earth a few times, but not the bait. Then, all of a sudden, she shifted position a little and pecked right down on the corn with the hook in it, the bait. For the second time that day I felt a strike vibrate through my hands. But the chicken missed the hook again and I jerked the bait out of her mouth. She didn't know what happened to it. She looked like, What in the world?

I repositioned the bait, and the hen started pecking around it again. I had to say something to Mama. I held real still and tried to talk in a voice that maybe a chicken couldn't hear. In my head I invented a voice that seemed like it was going to be all throaty and hoarse and animallike when it came out, but when it did come out, it didn't make any sound at all, not even a whisper, just a little bit of released breath and a wormy movement of my lips. I said, "Mama, I ain't fishing for chickens." Nobody heard it, not even me. The Plymouth Rock hit the bait a third time.

It wasn't possible to catch a chicken. I knew that. My daddy had convinced me. He said, "A chicken is dumb, but not dumb enough." So I knew it was impossible. But I also knew it had happened. I had the Plymouth Rock.

I jerked my pole skyward and set the hook hard in the chicken's beak.

The sound that rose up out of the chicken's throat was a sound that nobody who has never caught a chicken on a hook has ever heard. It sounded like chicken-all-the-way-back-to-the-beginning-of-chicken.

I was anchored to the porch, with the butt end of the pole dug into my groin for support. The heavy flopping squalling bird was hanging off the end of my line in midair. The sound didn't stop. The sound was like the fire siren in Arrow Catcher. As beautiful and as scary as that. It was like a signal. I thought it signaled danger and adventure and beauty.

I was screaming too, along with the chicken. I didn't even know I was screaming. I heaved on the heavy bird. The pole was bent double. I wanted to land the chicken. I wanted the Plymouth Rock on the porch with me.

I couldn't pick it up high enough. It was too heavy for me. It was up off the ground, all right, but I couldn't get it high enough to sling it onto the porch. The chicken was beating its wings and spinning in a wild circle. I held it there.

I heaved on the pole again. The bird swung up and around, but was still not high enough. It hit the side of the house and then swung back out into midair.

Mama came out on the porch and stood behind me. I knew she was back there, because I heard the door slap shut.

At first I didn't look back. I just stopped hauling on the chicken. I was still holding it up off the ground, though. I couldn't give it up yet, not all of it, even though I had stopped trying to land it.

Finally I did look back. The face of my mama, I thought, was the saddest face on this earth. It just had to be. I said, "Hey, Mama," real subdued, trying not to provoke her. I was still holding the chicken off the ground, and it still hadn't stopped making its noise. I said, "I been fishing for chickens." No use lying about it now.

I expected my mama to say, "I swan," like she always said when she meant "I swear." What she really said surprised me. She said she was a big failure in life. She said she was such a big failure in life she didn't see why she didn't just go off and eat some poison.

I eased the chicken down onto the ground. It got loose and scooted off toward the garage with its feathers sticking out.

Mama cut a switch off a crape myrtle and switched me good on my bare legs and went back inside the house. She lay across her bed on the wedding-ring quilt my grandmama Sugar gave her when she got married, with hers and Daddy's names sewed in a corner and a heart stitched around the names, and had herself a long hard cry. And so that part of it was over.

Some time passed. Some days and, I guess, some weeks. I watched my mama around the house. At night, after supper, and after she had wiped the table, she would do what she liked best. She would lay out on the table a new piece of cloth from Kamp's Low Price Store and pin to it a tissue-paper Simplicity pattern. She would weight the pattern down all around with pieces of silverware from the dark chest lined with green felt. The silver came from my mama's grandmama who lost her mind and threw away the family Bible and almost everything else and so left only the silverware, which she forgot to throw away. Mama would get the pattern all weighted down, and she would look around for a minute, in her sewing basket or in a kitchen drawer, and say, "Has anybody seen my good scissors?" She would find the scissors and bring them to the table and cut through the paper and the cloth. She would poke through her sewing basket. I saw the faded pin-cushion and the cloth measuring tape and a metal thimble and about a jillion buttons and the pinking shears.

She would lay down a towel to keep from scratching the dining room table and then heft the heavy old portable Kenmore onto it. She might have to thread the bobbin. She might lift the cloth to her nose and breathe its new-smell before she put it into the machine, under the needle, and on the shiny metal plate. She would touch the pedal with her foot.

Before any of this would happen, before supper even, my daddy would come home from work. I could hear the car pull into the drive and head around back of the house. He would get out of the car, and he would be wearing white overalls and a paper cap with the name of a paint store printed on it. He would smell like paint and turpentine and maybe a little whiskey.

Daddy would shoo the chickens back from the gate in the fence where the chickens would flock when they heard his car. He would open the gate and ease inside, real quick, before anybody could get out. I would watch him.

The chickens were gossipy and busy and fat and fine. Daddy would scatter shelled corn from a white metal dishpan and pour out mash for those that needed it and run well water into the troughs.

I always wished Mama would watch him do this. I thought that if she did she would stop thinking she was a big failure in life.

I went down the steps and into the chicken yard with him. He let me reach my hand into the fragrant dusty corn and pelt the old birds with it.

Then there was the part where the rooster attacks you. Every day I forgot it was going to happen, and then it would happen and I would think, Now why didn't I remember that?

It happened today, this particular day, I mean, a Tuesday and just before sunset. The rooster was on top of us. It hadn't been there before, and now it was all I could see, the red furious rooster. Its wings were spread out and its bones were creaking and clacking and its beak was wide open and its tongue was blazing black as blood. And the rooster's eye—it looked like it had only one eye, and the eye was not stupid and comical like the other chickens'. It seemed lidless and magical, like it could see into a person's heart and know all his secrets and read his future. And the feet—they were blue-colored, but blue like you never saw before except in a wound. And the spurs.

And then it was over. Today, like other days, Daddy kicked the chicken in the breast with the toe of his work shoe and it flopped over on its back. It righted itself and stood up and started pecking at the corn on the ground. Daddy walked over to the rooster and petted its neck. The bird made a stretching motion with its head like a cat.

Then there was the next part. We watched the rooster eat. Without warning, as we knew it would, it stopped eating. It stood straight up and cocked its head so far that the comb flopped over. It looked like somebody who has just remembered something real important.

Then the rooster took off. Any other flying chickens you see are all hustle and puffing and heaving and commotion and getting ten feet maybe, no matter how hard they work at it. This chicken could fly like a wild bird, like a peacock, maybe, or a wild turkey. There was nothing graceful about it, nothing pretty. It was just so amazing to watch. When the rooster flew, it looked like some fat bad child who has rung your doorbell and is running down the street away from your house, slow and obvious and ridiculous, but padding on any-way, uncatchable. It flew out and out, over the chicken-yard fence, over a little side yard where Mr. Love kept a goat, over the trailer the midgets lived in, out farther like a kite, over a house, and finally into the branches of a line of hardwood trees across the railroad tracks.

We went inside the house then, and Daddy went into the bathroom and came out after a long time with his new smells of Wildroot and Aqua Velva and his wet combed hair. The whiskey smell was a little stronger, a little sweeter.

After supper, and after the sewing machine was turned off and put away, Mama said, "Now all I have to do is hem it, and it'll be all done." She was on the sofa, so she sat up straight and held the dress up to her front and pretended like she was modeling it. Daddy was moving out of the room. He was weaving a little when he walked, on his way to the kitchen.

I looked at Mama. She had a pleased look on her face that made me think she thought she looked pretty. She did look kind of pretty.

I picked up the package the pattern came in. There was a color picture of two women on it. I said, "Where do these ladies live, Mama?"

She took the package out of my hand and looked at it with the same look on her face. She looked off somewhere away from my eyes and said, "I think maybe these two ladies live in New York City. They live across the hall from one another in a penthouse apartment. I think they just met up downtown by accident." She looked at me and smiled and handed the pat-tern package back to me.

I said, "What are they talking about?"

Mama said, "Hm." She took the package from me again and looked at it, serious. She said, "I think maybe, well, maybe the lady in the red dress is saying why don't we go somewhere real nice today. She's saying why don't they shop around a little and then maybe go to a picture show. They might even be talking about going to the opera, you don't know."

I tried to think about the opera, men in turbans and women in white-powdered wigs. The men carried sabers at their sides, and the women had derringers in their purses. I said, "I ain't studying no opera."

Mama laid the package down and put the new dress aside too. She started poking through her sewing basket for something, but then stopped without finding it. She had lost the look she had before.

I said, "Are you going to the opera?"

She said, "No."

I said, "When you put on that dress, you know what?"

She didn't answer.

I said, "You ain't going to look like neither one of those ladies." I don't know why I said that.

Mama got up from where she was sitting. She said, "Don't say *ain't*, Sugar. It will ruin your life." She got up off the sofa and went into the bedroom and closed the door.

Daddy came back into the living room. He was wobbly and ripe with whiskey. He said, "What happened to Mama?"

I said, "She's lying down."

He eased back into his chair and started to watch "Gilligan's Island" on the television.

I went to my room. I sat on the bed and let my feet hang off. I had to do something. I felt like I was working a jigsaw puzzle with my family. I saw my mama and my daddy and the chickens and the midgets and Mr. Love's goat and I thought I could never get it worked.

I started to fish for the rooster. Sometimes I fished with a handline, sometimes with a cane pole. The rooster never looked at my bait.

I fished every day, and every day I got older and the rooster didn't get caught. School started up again and I got new shoes. The leaves finally fell off the trees and I helped Mama rake them up in the afternoons. The rooster hated my bait. He couldn't stand to look at it.

I changed bait. I used raisins. I used jelly beans. I used a dog turd. You got to want to catch a chicken to bait a hook with dog turd. Chickens eat them all the time, no reason it wouldn't work. It didn't though.

I threw the cat in the chicken yard. I had ten hooks dangling off the cat, feet and tail and flea collar, everywhere you can put a hook on a cat. The rooster killed the cat, but it didn't take a hook. Too bad about the cat. You're not going to catch a rooster without making a sacrifice or two.

After a while fishing for the rooster and keeping Mama from knowing about it became like a job, like an old habit you never would think about breaking. All that mattered was that I fish for him, that I never give up, no matter how hopeless, no matter how old or unhappy I got.

Something happened then that changed things. It was Saturday. I got on my bike and pedaled from my house to the picture show in Arrow Catcher. There was always a drawing at the matinee.

Mrs. Meyers, the old ticket-taker-upper with the white hair and shaky hands and snuff-breath—she would do the same thing every time. She would take your ticket out of your hand and tear it into halves and tell you what a fine young man you were growing up to be and to hold onto your ticket stub, you might win the drawing.

I walked down the aisle and found me a seat up close to the front. I looked at the torn ticket in my hands, and the other seats filled up with people.

Mr. Gibbs owned the picture show, called it the Strand Theater. The lights were all on bright and Mr. Gibbs climbed up on the stage by a set of wooden steps around the side. He was huffing and sweating, waving his hands for everybody to be quiet. Like he said every Saturday, he said, "Be quite, boys and gulls, be quite, please." We laughed at him, and the underarms of his white shirt were soaked with sweat.

I watched Mr. Gibbs crank the handle of a wire basket filled with ping-pong balls. Every ball had a number on it. Mr. Gibbs would draw them out, one at a time, and put each one on a little cushioned platform with the number facing out to the audience, until he had four of them. He would draw them out slow and teasing and smiling. It was something he loved to do, you could tell. He would call out each number in its turn, real loud and exaggerated. He would say, "Fo-urrr," or "Nye-unn," and he would hold up the white ball and show everyone he wasn't cheating, and then he would put the ball on the cushioned stand. You had to like Mr. Gibbs.

Then it started happening. The first number he called out was the first number on my ticket stub. And then so was the second. It seemed impossible that the number in my ear was the same number as in my eye. It kept on being the same number, digit by digit, right down to the end. I had won the drawing.

I had never won anything before. One time I won a pink cake in a cakewalk. It tasted terrible and I hated it, but I ate all of it anyway, same night I won it. I had never won anything except that cake, so it was impressive enough to win the drawing.

But winning was nothing compared to the prize I was going to take home. I had won the Zebco rod and spinning reel from the Western Auto.

Mr. Gibbs was standing up on that little stage like a sweaty fat angel. He was giving his heartfelt thanks to the Western Auto store, homeowned and homeoperated by Mr. Sooey Leonard, and to all the other fine local merchants of Arrow Catcher who donated these fine prizes and made these drawings possible.

I went up on the stage. I climbed the same dusty wooden steps that Mr. Gibbs had climbed. I showed Mr. Gibbs my ticket stub. I was trembling. He shook my hand, and my hand was sweaty and slick against his manly palm and fingers. Mr. Gibbs asked me if I didn't think every single person in this fine audience ought to take his patronage to the Western Auto store and all the other fine local merchants of Arrow Catcher.

I said, "Yessir," and everybody laughed and clapped their hands.

Mr. Gibbs said what was I doing to do with my fine prize.

I said, "Go fishing," and everybody laughed again.

Mr. Gibbs said why didn't everybody give this fine young fisherman another round of applause, and so everybody did.

I don't know what was on the movie. I sat through it, and I watched it, with the fishing rod between my legs, but I didn't see it. I remember a huffing train and some wreckage, I remember an icy train platform and taxicabs and a baby growing up rich instead of poor. Barbara Stanwyck married John Lund, I remember that. Whatever was on the movie, one thing was all I was thinking about and that was that I was definitely going fishing, no doubt about it. The fish I was going to catch was as tall as me and had red feathers and was big enough and fine enough to ruin the life of every soul in Arrow Catcher, Mississippi.

I look back at the day I caught the rooster. I see the familiar yard, the fence of chicken wire. I smell the sweet fresh fragrance of grain and mash and lime and chickenshit and water from a deep well poured through troughs of corrugated metal. I smell creosote and the green pungent shucks of black walnuts under the tree. I see the trailer the midgets lived in and the goat next door. I see myself, a boy, holding the Zebco rod I won at the Strand Theater. The Zebco moves back, then whips forward.

The line leaps away from the reel, from the rod's tip. It leaps into S's and figure eights. It floats like the strand of a spider's web. At the end of the line I see the white fleck of sunlight that covers the hook: the bait, the kernel of corn. I watch it fly toward the rooster.

I look ahead of the corn, far down the chicken yard, and see the rooster. It seems to be on fire in the sunlight. For one second I lose my mind and believe that the rooster means something more than a rooster. I don't believe it long. I come to my senses and know that the rooster is a chicken, that's all. A very bad chicken. He is the same miserable wretched mean bad son-of-a-bitch that my daddy has called him every day of the rooster's life. I remember that the rooster is smarter than me, and faster and stronger and crazier. I remember that I am in the chicken yard with him and that he doesn't like me and that my daddy ain't home from work to protect me and my ass is in trouble, Jack.

I understand, at last, what the rooster is going to do. He is going to catch the bait in the air, like a dog catching a Frisbee. I can't believe what I am watching. The rooster has positioned itself, flat-footed, with its mouth open, its head cocked to one side. Until this moment I have not believed I would catch the rooster. I have meant to catch it, but the habit of fishing for it is all I have thought about for a long time. And now, in the presence of an emotion something like awe, I understand that the rooster is about to catch me.

It happens. The rooster, at the last moment, has to lurch a step forward, it has to duck its head, but it does so with perfect accuracy. The bird might as well have been a large red-feathered frog plucking a fly from the air. He catches the baited hook in his mouth.

I do not move to set the hook. There is no point. The rooster has been fishing for me for three years, and now it has caught me. I have become old enough to believe that doom will always surprise you, that doom is domestic and purrs like a cat.

The bird stands quiet with the bait in its mouth. The line droops to the ground from his chicken lips. I stand attached to him by the line. It is no help to remember that the rooster is a beast and without humor.

Then it does move. At first I thought the creature was growing taller. Nothing could have surprised me. I might have been growing smaller. Neither was true. I was watching what I had watched many times. I was watching the rooster take flight.

It left the ground. The hook was still in its mouth, attached to nothing. The rooster was holding the hook in its mouth like a peanut.

More than ever the bird seemed on fire. It flew out and out, away from me. The nylon line trailed it in flight. The sun shone on the rooster and on the line and told me that I was in big trouble and had not yet figured out how.

It flew over the chicken-yard fence, over the goat, over the midgets. It gained altitude. I watched the line be stripped in coils from my open-faced reel. The bird flew and flew, high as the housetops, and then the treetops, out toward the railroad tracks. I was a child flying a living kite.

It took me a minute to see what the rooster was up to. I had never seen him do this before. Just when he was almost out of sight, out over the railroad tracks and ready, I thought, to light in the hardwood trees, the bird seemed to hang suspended. It seemed to have hung itself in midair and to have begun to swell out like a balloon. I was holding the fishing rod limp in my hand and studying the rooster's strange inflation. The rooster, above the treetops, ballooned larger and larger. It grew large enough that I could distinguish its particular features again, the stretched neck and popped-out eyes, the sturdy wings and red belly feathers. Nothing about the appearance of the rooster made sense.

And then everything did. I was not looking at the bird's tail-feathers, as I should have been. I was looking him in the face. He was not growing larger, he was coming closer. I looked at my reel and saw that the line was still. The rooster had turned around in flight and was coming back after me.

I looked at him. The rooster had cleared the goat and the midgets. It was big as a goose, big as a collie. Its feet were blue and as big as yard rakes. I dropped the fishing rod into the dirt. I turned to the gate and tried to open the latch. I could hear the rooster's bones creaking and clacking. I could hear the feathers thudding against the air. My hands were clubs, the gate would not come unlatched. I pounded at the gate.

I heard the rooster set its wings like a hawk about to land on a fence post. The rooster landed on my head. It didn't fall off. I thought it might, but it did not. It clung to my scalp by its fierce toenails. I clubbed at the gate with my useless hands. The bird stood on my head, and its wings kept up their motion and clatter. I could not appreciate the mauling I was receiving by the wings for the fire the feet had lit in my brain. I tried to climb the gate, but my feet had turned to stumps.

The chicken yard was in hysterics, the Plymouth Rocks and Leghorns and blue Andalusians. I clung to the gate with the rooster on my head. I imagined flames the shape of an angry chicken rising from my head.

I screamed, and still the rooster held on. It drubbed me with its wings. My eyes were blackened and swollen, my nose ran with blood. I didn't care, so long as someone put out the fire in my scalp.

I got the idea that it could be put out with water. I gave

up at the gate and ran stumbling across the chicken yard.
Layers and pullets and bantams, all the curious and hysterical,
fanned away from me in droves. The rooster hung on.

I reached the hydrant hopeless. There was no hope of putting my head under the spigot while wearing the chicken.
There was a garden hose in the old garage, but it was of no
use. If I could not open the simple latch of the gate, there was
no chance I could retrieve the garden hose from its wall hook
and screw it to the spigot.

My mama was standing on the back porch watching. I
longed for the days when I was young enough to be switched
with crape myrtle. I saw her start to move toward me. She was
moving toward me but I knew she would never reach me in
time. Blood and chickenshit ran down the sides of my face
and into my ears. The wings kept up the pounding, and the
rooster's bones and ligaments kept up the creaking and clacking and clicking.

I had not noticed my daddy drive up, but now I saw his car
in the driveway. He left the car and was headed toward me.
He also moved in slow motion.

I left the spigot. My motion and my parents' motion had
become the same. They stood at the gate and pounded at it.
Their hands were clubs too and the gate would not open for
them.

I motioned for them to stay where they were. They saw that
I knew what I was doing. Something had changed in me. I
was not running now. The rooster was still riding my head.
I walked, purposeful, like a heavy bear through the chicken
yard.

And yet my steps were not heavy. My life was not ruined. I
could wear this chicken on my head forever. I could bear this
pain forever. In a year no one would notice the chicken but
myself. Then even I would not notice. My mama had believed
that spending your life in the place of your birth, absorbing its
small particulars into your blood, was ruination. I looked at
my parents beside the gate. My daddy held my mama in his
arms as they looked at me. My daddy had gotten the gate
open now but again I held up my hand and stopped him. I
knew now what I could give them. It was a picture of myself

that I would live the rest of my life to prove true: they watched their son wear this living crowing rooster like a crown.

They were proud of me. I knew they were. They were frightened also but pride was mainly what I saw in their faces as I kept them from helping me. They believed that my life would not be ruined. They believed that a man who has worn a chicken on his head—worn it proudly, as I was beginning to do—would never be a fool to geography or marriage or alcohol.

I stood tall in the chicken yard. My parents looked at me from the gate and I felt their love and pride touch me. They believed that a man and his wife with such a son could not be ruined either, not yet, not forever.

The rooster had stopped flapping its wings. It was heavy on me, but I straightened my back and did not slump. Now it balanced itself with more ease, it carried more of its own weight and was easier to hold. It stood on my head like an eagle on a mountain crag. I strode toward my parents and they toward me. The three of us, and the rooster, moved through the chicken yard in glory.

THE TALKER AT THE
FREAK-SHOW

The summer I was eleven a freak-show followed the Arrow Catcher Fair into town. The Fair itself was an annual event and very popular; motels filled up for miles in every direction. It was not uncommon for various sideshow-type attractions to set up in the shadow of the Fair to catch the overflow. A wild animal cage, a caricaturist, a boomerangist, two men and a horse who dived from a high platform into a vat of water—all at one time or another found space beneath the spreading cottonwoods and pecan and black walnut trees of the fair-grounds. Evangelists sometimes set up a tent or a booth, and once a gospel singer of great talent and pain stole the attention and hearts of spectators at the Fair.

Mama was opposed to my going to any such event, even a gospel singer or boomerangist, so a freak-show seemed out of the question.

After supper I didn't wait, I did what I knew would please Mama. I went around the table and stacked the plates and took them to the kitchen. Mama said, "Why, Sugar-man, *thank* you."

We had used paper napkins, but there was a stack of linen napkins in the sideboard. I took one from the top drawer and snapped it out smartly and held it draped over the open palm of my hand. With the other hand I brushed crumbs off the table into the napkin until the table was clean and then I stepped smartly past Mama to the trashcan in the kitchen and shook the crumbs into it. I recreased the napkin and put it back in the sideboard.

Good linen reminded Mama of trains, and the thought of

trains would sometimes soften her mood. She was thinking of black porters in starched white jackets, of Pullman cars flashing across snow-fields and through tiny nameless train stations at dawn and into great cities. She was thinking of soiled linens—sheets piled in the aisles of sleeper cars—and of tablecloths in the diner embossed with the Illinois Central emblem, or with the name of some train on the IC line, the City of New Orleans, the Panama Limited, the Loozianne. She loved to speak the names of those trains. She sang them to me in the night sometimes, sad sweet songs she made up about them. It was my lullaby since the beginning of my memory.

I closed the drawer of the sideboard and knew that she was thinking of the sweet noisy Amtrack from Chicago still carrying—in her mind, even though it was July—a skim of ice on its front cars and nosing southward to New Orleans and the Gulf of Mexico, and riding in one of its staterooms some beautiful lonely woman brushing her hair before a mirror. I wiped off the table with a damp sponge and had done all I could do.

I sat in the living room at one end of the sofa, where Daddy was watching tv. He left the room for a minute to go to the linen closet in the bathroom where he kept a bottle, and came back smelling sweet with whiskey, ripe in fact, since he had been sweetening himself all afternoon.

He sank into the other end of the sofa. After a while he said, "Have you seen this one before?" He meant the tv show that was on. It was called "A Special Musical Edition of The Love Boat."

I said, "Nosir."

Then as each actor crossed the screen he would tell me the actor's name. "That's Eddie Albert," he would say. "See that one?—that's Ann Miller. She used to be a great dancer."

There seemed to be dozens of them. He pointed out Ethel Merman, Pearl Bailey, even Duke Ellington. He said, "Each one of those fine actors is actually a great musician in his own right." He said that not a single one of them needed to be on television. "It's just a lark," he said. "They don't even need the money. For them the Love Boat is just one big party, like a vacation they get paid for taking." (In a strange way Daddy

seemed sincerely to believe everything that happened on television, at least that all the places were real, the geography. He
was convinced that Gilligan's Island and Fantasy Island were
charted on maps by those names, that Mayberry was a real
town in North Carolina. He was sure that the Love Boat was a
commercial ship on which a person could book passage.) He
said, "I wish I could afford to take that cruise someday, the
one with the musicians. I would like to shake each and every
one of those artists by the hand personally." He said he was a
lot like each of them, that he would tell them he knew their
hearts.

I said, "Can I go to the freak-show?" It was a mistake, I
should have waited for Mama.

Daddy looked at me. He said, "Did you hear one single soli-
tary word I spoke?"

Mama came into the room drying her hands. She said, "I
wish you wouldn't go to the freak-show, Sugar."

Daddy said to her, "Sugar here tells me he never heard of
Duke Ellington. Seems impossible, don't it? I guess Sugar is
just too busy talking about freak-shows to listen and maybe
learn a little something. Sugar's not aware of what all you can
learn by paying attention to conversation for once in his life."

Mama said, "You don't want to go to the freak-show, Sugar-
man. Those pathetic souls . . ."

Daddy said, "When I was your age I knew how to listen to
television and learn a few things. When I was your age I one
time slipped off from the house on a Saturday morning and
took the bus to Memphis. All by myself. And do you know
why?"

Mama said, "Gilbert . . ."

He said, "To see the late great W. C. Handy, that's all. I expect you never heard of the late great W. C. Handy, did you,
Sugar."

I said, "Not for a while."

He said, "I expect you never heard of Beale Street either,
did you."

Mama said, "The trash a sideshow like that will attract . . ."

Daddy said, "W. C. Handy was the Father of the Blues, that's
all W. C. Handy was. Just the Father of the Blues, for God's
sake."

Mama said, "Gilbert . . ."

Daddy said, "And the brilliant Sugar Mecklin never heard of him. Eleven years old and never heard of the late great W. C. Handy."

Mama said, "Gilbert . . ."

Daddy said, "And do you know why you never heard of him? Because you don't know how to watch television." He said, "Do you want me to tell you who W. C. Handy was? In your infinite wisdom are you willing to learn one more little thing?—like the identity of the Father of the Blues?"

I said, "You bet."

He told me that when he was a boy—Mama rolled her eyes, she couldn't stand this story—the late great W. C. Handy had a fifteen-minute television program from Memphis on WMCT at noon. "Alive and in person," he said. He said he would stay home from school pretending to be sick so he could watch the old man and listen to him play trumpet. "Me!—alive and young and in love with music, and W. C. Handy not even dead!"

Mama said, "You won't go to the freak-show will you, Sugar?"

I said, "All by yourself?"

Daddy said, "Eleven years old. All alone. All the way to Memphis. On the Greyhound bus."

Mama said, "I don't want you at that freak-show. I mean it."

I said, "*Beale* Street?"

He said, "Never heard of it, did you?" He went to the linen closet again and came back sweeter than ever. He told me the story of how he walked Beale Street like a king.

Mama gave up. She got up from her chair and walked to the big wardrobe in the hallway and came back with a large cardboard box filled with clothes given to her by a rich old Cajun woman who was dying.

Daddy didn't like for Mama to accept used clothes. He stopped telling me about his trip to Memphis. He said, "Mamzelle Montberclair is a hundred years old, Mama."

Mama took out a black silk dress with a huge black silk rose at the breast and held it up to her shoulders to model it.

Daddy said, "You don't want to wear the clothes of a woman a hundred years old." He added, "I don't care *who* she is."

Mama was sitting in an overstuffed chair that she liked. The box was in her lap and she had her feet tucked back under her. You could tell that she felt pretty. Was trying to feel pretty.

She said, "It's not *who* she is. Look at this dress, it's lovely. You could wear a dress like this to . . . why, anywhere on earth."

Daddy said, "*If* you was a hundred years old."

Mama put the black dress aside and pulled another, heavier piece out of the box. It was a cloth coat with a fur collar.

Daddy said, "It's an insult to me. I don't want to be seen with my wife wearing hundred-year-old-woman clothes."

I didn't like the turn the conversation had taken. I was willing to forget about the freak-show.

Mama smoothed the fur collar with her hand and then picked at something invisible in the perfect fur with her fingers.

Daddy said, "It looks like something Mamzelle caught under her sink."

Mama stopped fooling with the collar. She put her hands in her lap and sat still for a while. She said, "I wish you wouldn't talk to me that way, Gilbert."

I didn't know what to say. I said, "Beale Street?"

Daddy turned to me angrily. He said, "You going to *think* Beale Street. I'm going to Beale Street your bare butt you open your smart mouth to me one more time." He said to Mama, still in his angry voice, "Talk to you in what way?"

It didn't get much worse. There was no screaming. Daddy watched the rest of the special musical edition of "The Love Boat," but I could tell he didn't enjoy it. He got up and snapped off the television and left the room.

On the way to my room I passed the bathroom and saw that the door was open. Daddy was standing in front of the bathroom mirror with a glass of whiskey in his hand.

He knew I was there, watching him, but he didn't stop, he played it out anyway. He raised the glass slowly and held it in front of him. He kept one eye on the mirror and touched the glass to his lips and drank. He lowered the glass and watched himself feel the bite of the whiskey. He said, "Uhh." He was tragic and handsome. He rinsed the glass and put it back on the sink.

He turned to me and said, "So my young man wants to go to the freak-show, does he?"

I wished I had never heard of the freak-show. I wished I hadn't watched him drink the whiskey.

He said, "So you would like to go to the freak-show with your ole daddy, would you. Would you like that, Sugar-man? Would you like for your daddy to take you to the freak-show?"

I said, "Bye, Mama," when we went out the door, but Mama didn't answer.

We entered the fairgrounds by the main gate, beneath the usual long banner with red lettering: Welcome to the Arrow-Catcher Fair. I kept close to Daddy.

There were crowds of people milling around the grounds, but not much activity. We pushed through a line of people buying hot dogs and Pepsis and cut past the bandstand and across the area where The Great Spit would be held, a tobacco spitting contest. Men were stretching out rolls of butcher paper for accurate marking of the distance of the farthest propelled droplet. We went on, past booths and games of chance, through a roped-off area where the arrow-catching events were held, past the ass-kicking booth, which was deserted except for Wiley Heard, the one-legged coach of the local football team. (I don't know what he was doing there.) Another booth was being decorated with crepe paper streamers by ladies from St.-George-by-the-Lake, the Episcopal chapel near the fairgrounds.

And then we came to the freak-show. I had no heart for a freak-show, not even a good one. I thought of Mama at home, picking at the fur collar of Mamzelle Montberclair's coat and dreaming of trains crossing through the forests of Canada and China and all the other places where snow fell and geese flew and danger heightened and refined lives. And this freak-show was not a good one.

Mama had been right about who would be in the audience, violent stupid men some of them, with Mama's-boy names— Precious Mahoney, who weighed four hundred pounds and carried a kitchen chair and a pistol and a dog-whip with him wherever he went, like a lion-tamer, who sat on the kitchen chair now before the freak-show platform, like a wise fat sun-freckled toad, the sleeves of his sweaty shirt rolled up over his red arms; Brother Hot McGee, who smelled like a fried-chicken shack and once accidentally killed a man in an argument over whether a willow was actually a tree or a weed; Dr. Pudd'n DeBlieux, whose last name was pronounced "W" and who was drunk beyond belief, Arrow Catcher's only physician. There were also the Bunkies and Tooties and Bubbas and Alicks and a brainless blockhead of a child my age named Joseph of Arimathea who was at the freak-show with his blind granddaddy, who carved soap.

The freak-show itself was no better than its audience. For one thing it was situated near the old trestle that crossed the lake, down on the gray hard mud-flats. It was a dry year, so the lake was low, and the platform and the tent and the spectators stood on land that usually was covered with water. "Those pathetic souls," Mama had said, and she was right. No one but a person of that description could have exhibited himself on this unholy ground, which smelled of mussels and rotten shellfish and the regular stink of gumbo land.

And yet the scene—the freak-show and, I suppose, its spectators—brought to Daddy a life and vitality that could not have been predicted. Before, he had been tramping and dogged and determined to do this thing, to take his son to the freak-show in spite of a wife who was forever knowing best and advising sensibly. Now he was alert and amazed and humble before what he considered the wonder and the glamour and the magic of show business.

I looked at him in surprise; he had changed in appearance. He had been small and weasly and drawn and petty in his drunkenness and anger, and now he was childlike and beautiful and new in his small stature. His eyes, like his mouth, were literally wide open. I saw him in the shape of the child he must have been at my age, in Memphis, on Beale Street, in the clash and glare and dark beauty of whores and the dangerous black men he must have braved to walk that wide now-extinct street in search of a man I'm sure he never found, old tan man Handy, the Father of the Blues, and held in his child-hand only a return bus ticket and in his child-mind danger and distance and courage and strange honor. I looked at him in love.

I looked at the freak-show and tried to see it through Daddy's eyes. Without having words for this, I tried to see the spectators of the Fair as he must have seen them, doomed and tragic men, romantic as explorers for their hidden pistols and whiskey-ruined, sun-ruined faces and lives. I could almost see them through Daddy's eyes, almost know some true bad value in their lives—Alick, whose business was the Hocus Pocus Liquor Store, which had a straw-hatted spook on its electric sign; Tootie, whose car lot had a sign that flashed a giraffe and a dachsund—High Quality, Low Prices; W, the physician, who saved lives. I could almost believe in their reverse beauty as he believed in it.

I looked hard at the freak-show and tried to see what he saw.

The freaks had done what they could to make the show a gay and interesting-looking affair. The wooden platform was securely built, with new two-by-fours here and there to replace those that must have broken or rotted. The tent behind it, a long shallow rectangular affair, was ancient and faded and water-stained—and yet it too had been the object of someone's special care.

Along its front wall had been painted large caricatures of the freaks inside—Jo Jo the Dog-faced Boy, Fanny the Fat Lady, the Alligator Woman, Mitzi Mayfair (a midget lady), a fire-eater, a four-legged man (who I learned later was not traveling with the show). The original caricatures were old-fashioned things, but they had been touched up with fresh paint.

There was a podium at the left side of the stage with a large roll of bright yellow tickets on top of it and, on the front of the podium, a hand-lettered sign that said, Show Time Dusk Come One Come All One Dollar.

A line of light bulbs had been strung around the top of the canvas and were blazing with yellow light. There were floodlights at the foot of the platform. A million bugs had been attracted to the light. There were also three faded banners that must have been red at one time, drooped down on the canvas from the tops of three of the tent poles.

Daddy said, "Look at it, Sugar! Just look!"

Suddenly I was afraid to imagine the wonders he saw in this

tacky spectacle. I saw only bugs and bare bulbs and faded flags, old-timey cartoons on stained colorless canvas.

Then a man stepped through the folds of the tent and walked, aimlessly I thought, onto the platform and stood scratching himself as if he were alone. The suit he was wearing was formless, made of silk the color of snuff. I am sure it had never been washed or cleaned in any way. Wearing it, he looked like a man who has been dashed with brown paint that is sheeting from him in bags and tatters.

For a long time he made no movement at all except the slow motion required to smoke a cigarette. He stood slumped with his hands in his pockets. He drew on the cigarette until the tip was red and then exhaled the smoke, which rose into his right eye and caused him to squint hard. When the butt was tiny he took it from his mouth with his left hand and field-stripped it in his slow casual precise way and then scattered the tobacco bits on the platform beneath him. He stood slumped again in his snuff-colored suit.

At last he began to move. He shook his head like a man waking up on a park bench and remembering where he is. As he came more to life, he moved forward to the front of the platform and started to speak.

He said, "I am *honored* . . ." For a while he spoke in his incredible, lethargic way, nasal and northern, of some vague wonderment which was his own to possess, or that possessed him, that seemed responsible for his presence on this platform, in this suit, which now I saw (with of course no words to say this) as the filmy material of himself, his real flesh, and beyond flesh.

He talked on, sweat poured off his face, and more and more the suit seemed a fluid and essential thing. The bugs in the floodlights had multiplied into the billions. They soared around the lighted area. They converged on the floodlights and rose up into the dark sky. They formed a haze between the talker—which is what we called him later—and his audience, as thick as a beaded curtain, and the curtain rippled and changed and rattled as if it had been shaken.

He spoke of the humanity inside the tent behind him. "Jo Jo," he said, "Ohyeah ohyeah, Jo Jo the Dog-faced Boy"—he was singing now—almost a song, his voice—singing to us in the sweltering Mississippi evening in a sweat-soaked silk suit the color of snuff and the shape of bad rain—"found, oh Jesus, in the wilds of Australia, continent of gentleness and punished sin, and raised by a friendly band of marsupials, ohyeah ohyeah." It was a song that rattled (seemed to rattle) the limbs and fruit of the pecan trees around us.

And then he stopped. He took a snuff-colored handkerchief from his pocket and mopped at his face. He did not look at us now. He did not move, only looked at the platform beneath his feet. Sweat formed again on his face and dropped to the boards in a pool.

We stood waiting on him, men and boys in our sweat-soaked shirts, women (there were a few) with sweat caking the talcum powder to their necks.

The talker turned sidewise to the audience and looked away from us, back at the cartoons on the tent. I thought—or think now anyway—that he looked like a trainer who, confident and heedless, turns his back on a troupe of performing animals and is not afraid.

When he began again he said that inside this tent behind him, for the sum of a single paper dollar bill, we would see Fanny the Fat Lady, that the bikini she wore was a bedsheet, that once she had been thin as a wisp, "as lithesome," he said, "as smoke" and lovely, that she had loved, unwisely, a traveling man and now ate to soothe the pain of her loss, that her fat was a measure of her love. Honesty throbbed in his voice like a musical saw.

Belief and disbelief were the same creature in me. My eyes suddenly saw lights blazing and banners whipping, the wonderful parade, elephants and hooves and bright horns, tight-rope dancers and jugglers and clowns, all that Fanny and Jo Jo and Mitzi Mayfair stood for in my daddy's mind, dark dangerous bright Beale Street in Memphis, the whores and knives and pointy-toed shoes and Panama suits and pink convertibles and blue-plumed pimps and, somewhere, probably asleep in his old-man bedroom with a slopjar beside the bed and flowered wallpaper on the walls, and lying beside a gray-haired shriveled old wife in a flannel gown, the brightest most dangerous apparition of all the amazing street, the Father of the Blues!—ancient and foolish and toothless and blind, W. C. Handy, live and in person, with snuff-colored skeleton fingers to touch the valves of a sweet oiled horn, DeBlieux C. Handy, in the same city, on the same street, and not even dead.

The talker was singing again, every sentence. He described the Alligator Woman—alley-gay-tor, he pronounced it, sang it—her mossy scaly skin; he described the Giant—sad and gentle, tragically born in Lapland where, when he was a child, there was not one lap large enough for him to sit in, not even his own mama's; the hermaphrodite ("Lord," he said, "the embarrassment, born of the union of brother and sister, twin children, Hermes and Aphrodite Johnson of the Hill District of Pittsburgh, Pennsylvania, Lord I say don't look, for God's love, do not, when you walk inside that tent, do not cast eyes on what is too private, too sacred, too sad to be seen, one dollar, a single paper dollar bill"); and he sang of someone else, I forget who, *ee wolnks ee tolnks ees almos chewmann ee crawlzonis-belly like a rep-tile*

The magic of his song made me know, or believe, that the Love Boat was, in some way, an actual ship that carried a crew of actors and sailed from ports where my daddy might book passage and board and embark and find love. I thought he did know the hearts of Ethel Merman and Eddie Albert and the others, that if he shook them by the hand they would somehow recognize him as their own kind and welcome him aboard, that the world on shipboard was a world made for him, with music and dancing and kisses, and that because he had entered it, so could I, all good men and women could, where Mama could wear silk roses and fur-trimmed coats and speak with strangers of train rides across the frozen Ukraine.

Men in the audience were paying their dollars to go into the freak-show. I was frightened but ready to walk inside too, to view a spectacle that would mark me forever with some sign, outward and visible, as my father's child and thereby make known to all the world that I too might shake the hand of Pearl Bailey and Duke Ellington and be recognized and received into their company.

I saw Daddy fumble excitedly in his pocket. He pulled out a

small roll of bills and peeled one off and stuck the others back.

Suddenly I knew he was not going to let me go into the freak-show. Daddy said, "Go on home." I said, "Let me go in." He said, "Go home, you don't want to see no morphodite." I said, "Joseph of Arimathea is going in, let me go in, Daddy." He said, "Joseph of Arimathea has got to describe it to his blind granddaddy. I ain't blind."

Daddy paid his dollar and took a ticket from the man in the snuff-colored suit and went inside without me.

For a minute, maybe longer, I stood by the platform in disbelief and shame. People pushed by me and paid their dollars and followed Daddy inside the tent, even the blind soap-carver and his blockhead grandson.

At last I left the Fair, alone and running, past the arrow-catchers and the ass-kickers and the tobacco-spitters and the Episcopalians.

At home I took off my clothes, down to my underwear shorts, and pulled back the covers of the bed. I lay in the darkness beneath a sheet and a bedspread I didn't need in the July heat.

Mama came up the stairs and into the room and stood beside the door with the light behind her. She was wearing Mamzelle's coat—in this heat, a winter coat!—why not just the silk dress? I turned on my side away from her.

She said, "Is everything all right, Sugar?"

I said, "Yes." I tried to make my breathing sound normal.

She said, "How was the freak-show?"

I said, "Okay."

She said, "Are you sure you're all right?"

I was tired of trains through winter forests, of romantic cruises and silk and fur and alcohol, the misery of false geographies and populations of misfits.

Mama sat on the bed beside me and touched my bare back beneath the covers with her fingers. She said, "What happened?"

I said, "Nothing."

I thought of the talker at the freak-show. I hoped he would

say to Daddy, "Eddie Albert wouldn't know you. Ethel Merman wouldn't shake your hand."

Mama said, "Don't be too hard on your daddy, Sugar."

I said, "Did he really go to see W. C. Handy? Did he really walk down Beale Street like a king?"

She said, "Oh, Sugar-man . . ."

I turned over on my back and looked at her. She was sweating in Mamzelle's coat. Her face was covered with sweat and her hair was stuck to her neck and forehead.

She said, "Daddy thinks that all the world's magic is almost evolved out."

I thought of Roebuck Lake, its swamps and sloughs and loblollies and breaks of cypress and cane, its sunken treetops and stobs and bream beds and sleepy gar rolling over and over and over, its baptizing pools and bridges and mussels and mosquitoes and turkey vultures and, now in the drought, the gray flaking mud-flats and logs crowded with turtles and sometimes a fat snake yawning its tame old cottony mouth like a well-fed dog in a pen.

I said, "Is that what the freak-show is?"

She said, "Dirty miracles."

I said, "What about Mamzelle's coat?"

For a long time neither of us spoke again. I may have slept, I'm not sure. Then Mama was singing to me in a dry dead voice, sweating in the dry Mississippi evening. She must have been singing some made-up song about trains, but in my ears it was the voice of the talker at the freak-show, a song about friendly roving bands of marsupials, of giants in Lapland, of Hermes and Aphrodite, of wonderful geographies.

I said, "Mama, it ain't worth it."

She said, "I know, Sugar. I know. But, Lord, I just love him so."

SUGAR, THE EUNUCHS
AND BIG G. B.

One time when I was eleven—this was fifteen years ago, soon after my daddy first told me that wild bands of eunuchs run amuck in the Mississippi Delta—I spent the night with a friend named G. B. Junior. His daddy's name was Big G. B., and his mama was Sweet Runa, rhymed with tuna. Big G. B. had a houseful of guns, all kinds, pistols and rifles and muzzle-loaders and shotguns, even a blunderbuss with a bell-shaped barrel, and an illegal thing or two, grenade launchers and automatic rifles. He loved to show them to G. B. Junior's friends.

In fact, the guns were about the only reason G. B. Junior had any friends. He was fat and had a round snoutish nose with prominent nostrils. He would wrestle you to the ground and hold you with his fat and put his face into your neck or bare belly. He would make a grunting, rooting sound with his mouth and nose against your skin. He called this "giving pig." G. B. Junior was a mess.

Big G. B. would show us boys his guns and treat us grownup. He'd say, "I wouldn't show you men these here firearms if I didn't know I could trust you." Sometimes he would tell us, "Always remember, it's the *un*loaded gun that kills." He would look me and G. B. Junior in the eye and say, "Now do each and every one of you men get my meaning?" Sweet Runa, his wife, might holler out from the kitchen, "Explain your meaning to them, Big G. B." He'd give us a manly wink.

So it was a bunking party and I was in a big bed with G. B. Junior. I don't know why I couldn't sleep. I felt lonely all the time, that's one reason. I wanted to be home where I could hear my mama and daddy in the kitchen. I could stand anything I could hear—that's what I thought. Anyway, I couldn't sleep.

I lifted the comforter and sheet off me and slid my legs from under the covers. It was January and cold in the room. I sat on the edge of the bed and pulled on blue-jeans and a tee-shirt, no shoes.

I eased out of the room and down the hall toward the bathroom to take a leak. When I was finished I stopped outside the bedroom where Big G. B. and Sweet Runa were sleeping. There were no lights on in the house, but the moonlight was bright and I could see the two of them beneath the covers sweet as whales.

I went into the room and prowled a little. I poked through some bureau drawers and didn't find much. I found a box of rubbers in Big G. B.'s bedside table and took one to keep; it couldn't hurt.

There wasn't much else to do. I walked out of the bedroom and down the hall.

I started to go back to bed, but on second thought walked down to Big G. B.'s gunroom and snapped on the light at the wall switch.

Guns were on every wall, most of them behind glass locked up. The dark bright oiled woods of the stocks and butts made me love Big G. B. and Sweet Runa. The room seemed orderly and under control and full of love. There were deer heads and goat heads and a bear skin on the walls. The face of Jesus was made out of Indian arrowheads and spearpoints. There were boxes of dueling pistols on a low table and a great gray papery hornets' nest hanging on a hook from a ceiling beam.

I went to a chest-like table topped with rose-veined marble and opened the drawer. I knew what was in it. There were two green felt bags, heavy with their contents. I took out the first and loosened the drawstring and put my hand inside and ran my fingers through the bullets like a pirate through coins in a treasure chest.

I set it on the marble top. The second bag was heavier, the pistol Big G. B. called his three-fifty-seven.

I took it out of its bag and held it in my right hand and measured its weight. It was nickel-plated and had a handcarved grip with a nickel ring at the bottom. I pressed the release near the trigger-guard, the way I had seen Big G. B. do a hundred times, and the cylinder swung out with a soft metallic sound.

It was loaded with six cartridges. Daddy said one time Tex Ritter performed live and in person right here in Arrow Catcher, Mississippi, on the stage of the Strand Theater. Tex Ritter would sign your program. Daddy said he was just a little boy at the time and he asked Tex Ritter if he had any advice for somebody who wanted to break into show business. (I wondered why Daddy would ask a question like that.)

I snapped shut the cylinder of the pistol with one hand, like a policeman, and it clicked into place. I used both thumbs to cock the hammer. I pointed the barrel at the bearskin on the wall and said, "Blammo," and then eased the hammer back down. (I don't know what Tex Ritter answered.)

I stuck the big revolver inside the front of my pants and walked out the gunroom door. I walked down the hallway and into the kitchen and right out the kitchen door and let the screened door slap shut behind me. It was freezing cold. Before I could get down the splintery frosty steps and out of the stiff grass of the backyard, my feet were numb.

Nobody was on the streets. I felt invisibility grow in my freezing bones.

I walked past the gin and past Runt Ramsey's house. I walked past the lightplant and past the firehouse where Hydro Chisolm, the marshal's grown son, shot stray dogs and blew the fire whistle, fire or no fire, and sometimes chased cars. I walked beneath the legs of the water tower and past a blind man's house, Mr. O'Kelly, who was sitting on his porch in the middle of the freezing night carving soap. A ventriloquist's dummy was sleeping in his lap. I crossed the railroad tracks at Scott Butane and from there I could see my house. The lights were on, as I knew they would be, no matter how late.

I walked into the sideyard, outside the kitchen window, and stood beside a line of fig trees. I was out of sight of the midgets, in case they were awake. They lived in a trailer on the other side of the house and worked construction on the pipeline. Mavis Mitchum, a lady who sucked her skirt, lived on this side. My bare feet were numb, and I could scarcely feel the frozen dirt beneath them.

I could see Mama and Daddy in the kitchen. Mama was wearing a quilted robe and looked like a witch, the way she looked when Daddy was drinking. Daddy wore white painter's overalls and a billed cap all day and then got dressed up to drink. He was wearing his salt-and-pepper suit and a fresh starched shirt and his favorite tie, with a horsehead painted on it, which he got long years ago when he was a boy and visited the winter circus in Sarasota, Florida, and fell in love with a woman who swallowed things, swords and fire.

Daddy had propped a square mirror in the kitchen window. On the counter were four half-pints of Early Times and four shot glasses. (He called this "shooting fours.") Mama was saying something to him, I knew what. She was saying to him that he was an artist, that he was special and perfect and magic, that his pain was special. She was telling him she wanted to carry his pain for him. I had heard it a hundred times, she meant every word. In front of the bare fig trees I grieved and celebrated my invisibility.

Daddy was looking into the mirror. Sometimes he would cut his eyes to it, quick, and glimpse himself there by surprise. Then he would stare at himself full face and turn his head, real slow, to catch another angle. He was tragic and handsome. He was dreaming of the woman who swallowed things. Mama was telling him that if his heart had to break she wanted it to break inside her own chest.

Daddy filled one shot glass from one bottle and then the next from the next bottle, and on to the end, until four drinks had been poured from four bottles into four glasses. He filled a larger glass with Coca-Cola from a quart and put it on the sink too.

He lifted the first shot in his hand and checked the mirror. Mama looked a hundred years old in her love for him. He drained the whiskey from the glass and set it back on the counter. He chased the drink with Coca-Cola. He looked into the mirror again. He was handsome and manly and tragic and fine. He was the Marlboro Man of alcoholism. He drank each of the four shots of whiskey in the same way.

I took Big G. B.'s three-fifty-seven out of my pants and pulled back the hammer with my aching cold thumbs and held the pistol in both hands.

The sound of the gun might as well have been Niagara Falls, it was so permanent and loud and useless.

A column of fire a foot long jumped out of the pistol's muzzle. The window I had shot through disappeared in one piece, glass and wood. Even the screen dropped straight down in front of me. When I fired the second shot I looked at my mama and believed that she was all women in the world, beauty and grief, and at the same time nobody at all, as shadowless and invisible as myself beside the white bare limbs of the fig trees. Then the lights were out and I was alone in my invisibility.

I walked out of the yard with the pistol still in my hand, swinging at my side, and went back to Big G. B.'s the same way I had come. The blind man was still carving soap, the dummy was awake now, had opened his eyes. Joseph of Arimathea was the dummy's name.

Neither of the shots had hit my daddy. I had missed him both times. I heard the siren of Big'un Chisolm's car just as I stepped inside Big G. B.'s back door and felt my feet start to thaw out. I put up the pistol and the cartridges and I slipped back into bed beside G. B. Junior. My body and my heart were saying, crying, *I want I want I want I want*

Joseph of Arimathea told the marshal I was the one fired the shots. The soap-carving blind man agreed with him. I heard this from the men talking at the Arrow Cafe. They were big talkers and big laughers and they acted like it was a joke and told me what a fine boy I was and don't worry about a thing, they all knew better than to believe a word those two dummies said, but there was nothing funny about it to me. I'll tell you why. Mavis Mitchum—the neighbor who sucked her skirt— she told on me too. She said she was up late watching for eunuchs and saw me. (She agreed with Daddy about the eunuchs. She said they sing and dance at Episcopal baptizings. Mavis Mitchum was a mess her own self.) Hydro saw me too, said he did. Hydro had a big head and wanted to be believed. He swore to his daddy he would never chase another car if some-body would please believe him, it was Sugar Mecklin who did the shooting he said, he saw me.

Big'un, the marshal, didn't believe any of them, least of all his own poor son Hydro. Big'un apologized to Daddy, and even to me. He made Hydro apologize. Big'un said it was bad enough to live in a town full of freaks (oh, he was hard on Hydro) let alone be accused by them. Daddy said, "It don't matter, Big'un." Big'un said, "I just wouldn't want you to think a whole townful of freaks has turned on your boy." Daddy said, "I know that, Big'un, it ain't everybody who's against us." Big'un was relieved. He said, "You so right, Gilbert. The mid-gets, for example, ain't said a word."

I was sick with grief. I cried all the next day and Mama held me and told me Daddy was fine, just fine, you hush, Sugar, he's not hurt one bit. It didn't help. I still couldn't stop. I lay on my bed in my room, but I couldn't lie still. I walked out in the yard and threw corn to the chickens. Nothing helped.

I wanted to confess to Daddy. I walked through our house and looked at all the things that told me he was alive. I looked at the closet full of empty whiskey bottles, I stirred them with my hand and made them rattle and clank. I read their labels and fondled their shapes. I held them up to the light, one and then another, and looked at the small drops of amber fluid that collected in the corners when I tilted a bottle to one side. I unscrewed the caps and tasted the fluid on my tongue and knew that this was the only magic that kept him alive and in love with the sorry likes of me.

People were in the kitchen. A party started that day around the bullet holes and lasted a month. People loved Daddy for being shot at. The Communists did it, somebody said, the Klan did it, jealous husbands and heartbroken women and politicians and "the money men" did it—the law, the church, the blacks, the Indians, even the Iranians—no suggestion was too outlandish—and Daddy and Mama didn't deny one possi-bility. There were a million good reasons a man as fine as my daddy might be shot at.

I went in Daddy's bedroom and opened the drawers of his

chest. I looked in his shirt drawer and picked up a shirt and held it to my face and breathed in the smell, the fragrance of Daddy's flesh that could never be washed out. It was whiskey and paint and Aqua Velva and leather and shoe polish and wool and peppermint. I closed that drawer and opened others. In the deepest drawer I reached in and searched with my hand, behind the underwear and the rolled socks—I knew what I was looking for—until I found the candy, the peppermint puffs that he hid there, the light unbelievable airy candy that melted on the tongue, as if it had never been there, and left only the taste, the sweet aroma that was always with Daddy. I don't know why he hoarded peppermint.

I looked between his mattress and box springs and found the cracked leather folder with the brass zipper. I opened it and took out the old Tex Ritter program with the faded-ink autograph. There was a full-face picture of Tex on the front, a black and white drawing of him wearing his big hat and smiling his big smile. "For Gilbert Mecklin, your friend, Tex Ritter," the autograph said. There was also a ticket in the folder, faded, torn across the center, with the words Ringling Brothers Circus on the stub. And there was a picture of Elvis Presley, an eight-by-ten glossy with Elvis' signature in the corner. There was a triangular tip of steel—it might have been a swordpoint. I believed that it was, I believed it had belonged to the woman who swallowed things. I put the swordpoint in my pocket and stuck everything else back in the folder.

I went to Daddy's closet and knew where to look for the suit. Not even Mama knew about the suit. I had found it by accident a year before.

Deep in the closet, back behind his shotgun, behind the rubber hip-waders and the canvas jackets, behind the croquet set with its wire wickets and slender-handled mallets and wooden balls with bright stripes, which he had bought drunk and had never taken out of the box or allowed Mama to set up, behind the box of souvenirs from the junior high school he had dropped out of—a script from a play called "The Beauty and the Beef," a boutonniere he had worn to a dance— lay the suitbox I was looking for.

I lifted the box out of the closet—white sturdy cardboard—

and put it on the floor of Daddy's bedroom. The house was full of people, more and more of them, looking at the bullet holes and congratulating Daddy. People were laughing and happy, whiskey bottles and ice and glasses were clinking. I lifted the top off the large rectangular box and laid it aside. I knelt on the floor in front of the box and lifted out the airy tissue paper, a piece at a time, away from the cloth of the suit.

The suit was cheap—thin and shiny, almost brittle, and there was no lining. There were a million loose threads in the seams. It was a suit jacket studded with rhinestones. The pants had a double row of rhinestones down either leg. I lifted the jacket from the box and held it in my fingers to test its incredible light weight.

I learned to cry with no sound. I could hear Daddy in the kitchen, with Mama and their friends. I could tell by the way he talked and laughed that he was dressed in his Sarasota tie with the painted horse's head. I knew that Mama was glowing with pride and joy and grief.

I put on the jacket and stood looking at myself in the door-length mirror on the closet. I thought of the woman who swallowed things. I thought of trapeze dancers and jugglers and freak-shows. I thought of Tex Ritter and of lariats and spurs and chaps. I thought of a man my daddy had known when he was a boy, who carried with him a saddlebag full of knives and another saddlebag full of harmonicas. He told me, "Sugar, I would die to play Orange Blossom Special on one of those harmonicas on stage." He said his favorite musicians were a group called the Harmoni-cats, which featured a dwarf with a harmonica three-feet long. He said, "I would live forever if I could throw those knives." He said, "If I could throw those knives, I would name them, each one. I would name one Boo Kay Jack, I would name one Django. I would throw them and I would watch the bright brave frightened face of a beautiful woman as it sailed end over end toward her—one knife and then the next and the next—until every knife was quivering in the board next to her sweet bare body and her perfect figure was outlined in steel." I was wearing the rhinestone-studded coat of my daddy, which was too big for me, and I was looking at myself in the mirror. The coattail hung down to my thighs, the sleeves covered my hands. Rhinestones ran the length of the sleeves, they outlined the lapels. I turned my back to the mirror and looked over my shoulder. I read the words spelled out in rhinestones on my back: *Rock 'n' Roll Music*. I thought—dreamed, somehow, although I was awake— that knives were being thrown at me, that harmonica music was being played. I thought I was riding horseback, behind somebody else, a man, that I was holding onto him, my arms around his waist, and that the horseman was insane and smelled of pepperment and whiskey and that he dug the horse's bloodless sides with silver spurs and was Death made flesh and was somehow also my daddy and mama and Tex Ritter and everybody else in Arrow Catcher, Mississippi, and that there was a voice in the wind and in the horse's hooves and it told me that we lived, all of us, in a terrible circus geography where freaks grow like magic from the buckshot and gumbo, where eunuchs roam the Delta flatscape looking for Episcopalians. I didn't know why I had shot at Daddy. I only knew I wanted to confess to him, to have him know that I knew he was magic and that I loved him, that I wanted to drink whiskey and be like him, to find a woman who swallowed swords and fire, to marry a woman like my mama, who could grow ugly with love. I wanted to confess my betrayal of Daddy to the midgets, so the last freaks in town might know and not think well of me. Nobody caught me that day, nobody came into the bedroom from the kitchen. I took off the jacket and replaced the tissue paper and folded the suit and hid it away again in the box, far back in the closet.

I was insane until April, when the eunuchs came to Arrow Catcher looking for St. George. I poached pigeons in the belfry of the Baptist Church (it was Daddy's favorite kind of hunting) and with a tennis shoe swatted down the warm fat feathery ovals, with amazed eyes and all their bustle and clutter and complaint, purple and gray and brown and white and with glittery heads. I peeled off their feathers and skin and took out their insides and spread them in front of me. I wanted to live in my daddy's skin, behind his rib-cage, to share his heart and lungs and liver and spleen. I wanted to confess to Daddy, but I could not. I cooked the pigeons over fires in the woods near Roebuck Lake, and ate them, mostly raw. I chanted *I want I want I want I want.* I squatted on the lake-bank, or in the pigeon-fragrant dark of the church loft and imagined wild bands of roving eunuchs galloping the Mississippi roads and flatwoods, clattering across bridges and through pastures, skirting the edges of small towns. I thought of farmers with rifles on the lookout for them like wild dogs among the livestock. I looked for my own face among the eunuchs.

I ran a low fever every day for months, and frightened my mama with my crying, which I could not stop. She was afraid for me, and Daddy drank, and I spent the night almost every night with friends, and finally with only one friend, G. B. Junior—and not really with G. B. Junior, with his daddy. I spent as many nights as I could with Big G. B. It may have been Mama's idea, to get me away from the drinking and the loud bullet-hole parties—I don't know whose idea it was. Big G. B. invited me to go places with him, especially out to his farm, which he called Scratch-ankle. He let me drive his pickup through the cattlegaps, we shot a .22 pistol at dead tree stumps. I was not afraid of the pistol. I shot accurately and he congratulated me on my aim. G. B. Junior was never invited to go with us.

Sometimes Sweet Runa would make Big G. B. take him with us, but it never worked out. G. B. Junior said he hated the stupid farm, he said the pistol shots hurt his ears, he said the pickup made him carsick. Big G. B. said, "Well, Runa, if he don't *want* to go . . ." So it was always the two of us. Sometimes we would check the horses, sometimes Jabbo Deeber, the black man who ran the farm, would take us to a honey tree and we would scoop out honey in the comb and suck it off our fingers and dodge the angry bees. Sometimes the three of us—Jabbo and Big G. B. and me—would pinch Red Man out of a foil pouch and I would end each day dizzy with joy.

Big G. B. knew who shot at my daddy. He didn't tell Sweet Runa, he didn't even tell me—I just knew he knew. He started keeping me, like I was his child. I wished I was his child.

On the first day of turkey season, in April, I was spending Saturday night with Big G. B. to go hunting early the next morn-

ing. Even Mama believed I was getting better in Big G. B.'s
care. I had stopped crying and running fever and poaching
pigeons. I had put back some of the weight I had lost after the
shooting. Daddy was still the town hero for getting shot at.
People bought him drinks, gave him tickets to football games,
asked his advice on things he knew nothing about. He dressed
up more and went to work less. He drank whiskey in front of
the mirror and spoke of taking a trip to see the winter circus,
which he said had been moved to Venice, Florida. I held onto
the swordpoint, I ate from his stash of peppermint, I wore his
Rock 'n' Roll suit.

And then, on that Sunday morning, the first day of the season, when the rain was lashing the windows and the abelia
hedges and I was awake at four o'clock and sitting at Big
G. B.'s kitchen table eating Rice Krispies and milk while Sweet
Runa and G. B. Junior slept, I brought out Daddy's swordpoint and laid it on the table. I laid out a few peppermint
puffs. I told him about the Tex Ritter program and the Rock
'n' Roll suit. I told him about Django and Boo Kay Jack and
the saddlebag full of knives and the one full of harmonicas. I
told him about the woman who swallowed things and about
shooting fours and Mama's housecoat and the pigeons. I told
him Daddy was magic.

Big G. B. said, "Your daddy ain't magic."

I said, "He ain't?"

He said, "Naw, there ain't any magic."

I said, "What about the blind man's dummy? Is Joseph of
Arimathea magic?"

He said, "Get your shotgun, Sugar."

I went to the corner near the stove and took my shotgun by
the barrel. I got my shell bag and looked at Big G. B. to see
what he was thinking. His face didn't tell me. I stood by the
kitchen door holding the shotgun and shells. I said, "Is Joseph
of Arimathea magic, Big G. B.?"

He said, "There ain't no magic. Magic is the same as sentimental. Scratch the surface of sentimental and you know what
you find?—Nazis and the Ku Klux Klan. Magic is German in
nature and evil and not real. Scratch magic, Sugar, and you're
looking for death."

I said, "You already know, don't you."

He said, "No man is going to get mad at his boy for taking a shot at him, Sugar."

This was the first time the shooting had been spoken between us. He said, "Shooting to kill is what a boy is supposed to do to his daddy, Sugar-man."

We went out the kitchen door together into the morning darkness, both of us carrying unloaded shotguns and the shell bag clicking between us. The rain was whipping through the porch screens and the floor was slick. We ducked out the screened door and down the steps and into the pickup. We slammed the doors and wiped rainwater off our faces. Sweet Runa and G. B. Junior were awake, trying to get G. B. Junior dressed to go with us.

Big G. B. didn't want to take him. He started up the engine. He said, "Sweet Runa is not a bad woman, Sugar. I want you to know that." Sweet Runa was shouting something to us from the back door, but we couldn't hear. Big G. B. shifted into first gear and we pulled out of the yard. I didn't say anything. He said, "And your daddy is not a bad man. He truly ain't." He was going through the gears of the truck now and his feet in the big boots covered his whole side of the cab floor. I looked back through the rear window and saw Sweet Runa and G. B. Junior standing in the yard in the rain. I said, "Big G. B., sometimes I hate myself so much." He slowed the truck and pulled to a stop. He started turning around to go back to the house. He said, "I just try to keep an open mind about Joseph of Arimathea."

So now G. B. Junior was in the front seat of the pickup too, surly and sleepy and unhappy and silent. Big G. B. and I were wearing the two camouflage ponchos and G. B. Junior was wearing a Day-Glo yellow slicker his mama had put on him. Big G. B. told him he couldn't wear a yellow raincoat in the woods, he would look like a fool. G. B. Junior said don't worry, he wouldn't wear it to a fucking dog fight and said he hadn't brought his shotgun, he wasn't going hunting. Big G. B. said don't use that word and what did he mean he wasn't going hunting, what was he doing in the truck if he wasn't going hunting. When we parked near the Arrow Cafe, G. B. Junior opened the truck door and stepped out into the rain and took off the Day-Glo raincoat and threw it into the bed of the pickup. Big G. B. said what did he want to do that for. I knew none of us would see the turkey woods that morning.

Hunters from all around Arrow Catcher were in the Arrow Cafe. Everybody was in camouflage and hip-waders and rain-gear, a dozen or more men. The linoleum was slick with rain that had blown in and had been tracked in, and Miss Josie, who ran the cafe, had thrown a couple of blue towels on the floor to soak up the water. Some of the men were at the counter and others were at tables or in booths, eating sausages and eggs and biscuits. Miss Josie was bringing extra gravy. A couple of men were having shots of whiskey with their coffee. The rain was lashing the streets and blowing like sheets on the line across the streetlights. G. B. Junior was soaked through, because he had taken off the raincoat. It was hard to think of a child as lonely and unhappy as G. B. Junior, or one as happy as I was. There were guns and ammunition belts everywhere, propped against the counter, leaned in corners, draped across tables and barstools. I thought of Tex Ritter on the little stage of the Strand Theater in Arrow Catcher, the way he looked on the program and the way Daddy had described him. I thought of my daddy as a boy in that audience, sitting on a hard chair down front and looking up at the big horse and the lariat and Tex Ritter's six-guns and boots and spurs and hat. I believed that my daddy and I were somehow the same person, that I had visited Florida and loved the woman who swallowed things. I believed that when I cried in my heart *I want I want I want I want* that I was speaking, crying, in my daddy's voice, saying what he meant to say when he dressed in secret in his Rock 'n' Roll suit and watched himself drink whiskey in the mirror.

We looked for a place for three people to sit in the Arrow Cafe. Big G. B. made Runt Ramsey change to another seat at the counter so there were two empty stools together near the rear. I sat on one of the stools and could see through the low window into the kitchen. A large black woman in an apron was flipping hotcakes and cracking eggs into a bowl. I loved the turkey hunters in the Arrow Cafe. I loved Miss Josie, who owned it. I loved Big G. B., who gave me love without pain. Big G. B. told G. B. Junior to sit on the other stool at the counter with me, but G. B. Junior wouldn't do it. He said he wanted to sit on the floor next to the jukebox. Big G. B. said, "Oh, got-dog, son," and went over and tried to talk him into sitting at the counter. He still wouldn't. He wouldn't even look at his daddy. He was fat as lard and shivering and drenched and angry and cold but he would not come up to the counter. I knew how much he hated me. I didn't care. I was glad he wouldn't sit at the counter. Some people in a booth told G. B. Junior come on over here, they had plenty of room if he wanted to sit with them. He wouldn't do that either. Big G. B. said, "Well, don't meddle with the jukebox." G. B. Junior said, "I ain't studying no fucking jukebox." Big G. B. pretended not to hear.

Big G. B. came to the counter and sat beside me—this was why I was glad for the empty seat. He put his big hand on my left shoulder and squeezed it. Miss Josie poured me a cup of coffee, because I was with Big G. B., and then looked in the direction of G. B. Junior on the floor and decided against asking if he wanted a cup, it was too much trouble. I felt like a king. In the midst of these men and their camouflage and, in my nostrils, the smell of coffee cooking and breakfast and whiskey and the fragrance of wet rubber raingear and canvas and in this room full of breached firearms and the click-click of ammunition in the pockets of these men—in my own pockets—and the fine low sound of manly laughter and good southern whiskey voices, I felt for the first time free of my daddy, his magic if there was magic. I felt it even now, when it was hardest to know which was Daddy and which was me, when I wasn't sure just who had sat in the Strand Theater and heard a whiskey-voiced cowboy sing rye whiskey rye whiskey rye whiskey I cry if I don't get rye whiskey well I think I will die. Even when it was hardest to believe that it was my daddy and not myself who remembered Sarasota and longed for Django and Boo Kay Jack and loved the music of Spike Jones and the Harmoni-cats and the dwarf with the three-foot harmonica, and Daddy who dressed in secret (as I did now myself) in a rhinestone suit and ate peppermint puffs—I felt free of him, free to feel hatred if that came to me, and resentment and pure anger where I thought there should be acceptance and awe and love. I was free of Daddy's shooting fours, would never have to aim a pistol at anyone ever again, never have to know or care why I shot at him in the first place, never have to confess to him those evil seconds and know the pain it would inflict in his heart and in mine.

I was sitting beside Big G. B. and he was pouring milk into my coffee and a drop of whiskey from a flat bottle into his. I looked out the big window and saw the rain lashing at everything, at the steel awning in front of the Arrow Cafe, the sidewalks gleaming with reflected light, the pickups with gunracks and STP stickers and water standing in the beds, and the alley, its slick brick street where somebody had piled mattress boxes, and I saw the van drive up. I could see it out the window, blue and extra long, with lots of seats in it. It was filled with grownup men in suits—I could see them already—eight or nine of them lined up in rows in their seats. The lights of the van shone through the sheeting rain, yellow and wonderful and unexpected in the dark morning. I watched the van park and sit with its motor running and the lights still on. Nobody got out. Nobody was looking at it but me. I kept watching, felt strange and frightened. I leaned on my stool far to the side so that my shoulder touched Big G. B.'s sleeve and allowed my heart to fill up with love for this big man, and for all these men who were not my daddy.

G. B. Junior had gotten up from his place on the floor and had pulled the jukebox out from the wall. He was groping around in the oily dust behind it for the cord, he wanted to plug it in. Miss Josie saw him and walked from behind the counter to where he stood. I could tell she didn't want to scold him in front of everybody, especially not in front of his daddy, or in front of me. I could almost feel sorry for G. B. Junior. He was trying to stick the plug into the wall socket.

A spray of rainwater and cold April wind caused Miss Josie and everybody else to look at the front door, which had opened. G. B. Junior went ahead with what he was doing and plugged in the jukebox. He started going through his pockets

for a quarter, but he didn't have one. I looked at the door too.
I expected to see whoever had been out in the van, the men in
suits, but it was not them.

It was Daddy who came in the door. He was a little out of
breath, not from running. His face was streaming with rainwater. He was wearing a plastic raincoat and a billed cap, so
wet it stuck to his head. The men in the cafe cheered when
they saw him, Runt Ramsey and Red Raby and Grease Foley
and Billy Corley and Jimmy Scallion, everybody. He was still
the town hero for getting shot at.

He was looking around the room, looking for me. I made
myself small so he might not see me. Men slapped him on the
back, offered him coffee and whiskey, which he didn't notice
just now. G. B. Junior stopped meddling with the jukebox and
looked at Daddy, with love I thought. I wondered why G. B.
Junior and I couldn't swap daddies.

Only Big G. B. didn't look up. He seemed to know it was
Daddy and that Daddy knew something or had something or
disproved something that might change everything. Miss
Josie's smile lighted up the room when she saw Daddy. He
didn't notice. He walked across the blue towels on the floor
and stopped and looked around until he found me.

I could see through the cheap plastic raincoat, of course, to
the paint-stained overalls and the flannel shirt. And yet I half-
expected to see that Daddy was wearing the Rock 'n' Roll suit.
He looked handsome and certain and hopeful, the way I
thought he might look in the rhinestones. I looked at his face
and saw that he was not drunk yet, maybe still sick with a
hangover, it was hard to tell. We faced each other and I felt
emotions come into my heart that I didn't want. I saw myself
with Daddy when I was six years old. I was sitting in a low tree
in our yard, maybe six feet off the ground, and Daddy was
painting the tree blue. He dipped carefully into the paintcan
with a brush and then spread the bright enamel evenly over
the bark, trunk, and branches. There was sweet magic in the
combined fragrances of enamel paint and mimosa blossoms.
The limb I sat on swayed and threatened to give way. I loved
the danger and the blue tree. Daddy said, "I hope this don't
kill it. The yard needs the color, though." I had believed in

the Arrow Cafe that I had become another man's child, that because I had fired his .22 pistol into tree stumps and had driven his truck through the cattlegaps and fished his ponds and lain on his floor in his den in front of his television set and fallen asleep and been carried in his arms to a warm bed and had loved him that all my terrible past had not really happened, that I had never been born into the family of a drunkard, handsome and tragic and fine as any man who ever walked across a movie screen, and that I had never learned from my mama that Daddy was magic and should be worshipped until she and I and everyone else who loved him grew ugly and pure and mad with love, and that the only control we could expect in our lives was exactly what we needed most, blue trees and pigeon suppers and lonely secrets in the backs of drawers and closets.

I turned on the barstool and held Big G. B.'s arm with both my hands. I knew Daddy had come for me. I didn't want to go. I was afraid to love him again, and yet I already did love him, I had never stopped loving him, even when I hated him. I held on tight to Big G. B. I cut my eyes toward G. B. Junior and read his hatred of me. No one else in the Arrow Cafe cared about hatred; everyone else was in love with my daddy. They loved him—not, as I had thought, simply because he had been shot at, but because he truly was in some way pure, in some way perfect, as they knew they would never be—as I knew I would never be—in some way special, as Mama had known he was and had given up her life and beauty in wonder of, and that nothing he had ever done—his drunken violence and self-pity, his bullying and meanness and pettiness—was unforgivable, nothing too terrible to embrace. I had no words for any of this at age eleven, I hardly have them now, fifteen years later.

All the men wanted Daddy's attention. All asked about him, asked to do things for him. He did not ignore them, but he was not interested either. I was still clinging to Big G. B., and Big G. B. had laid his big hand over both of mine.

Daddy came squishing and squelching and squeaking across the linoleum in his rubber boots. He stood beside me at the barstool. He said, "Sugar, those men out in the van—do you know who they are?" He might have been giving me a gift, might have been afraid I was too young to know its value, too small to accept it. I shook my head to say no. He said, "It's the eunuchs. I called Sweet Runa and she told me y'all were down here. I wanted to let you know."

I let go of Big G. B.'s arm. I didn't know what to do with my hands. I put my face in them and put my head down on the counter, the way Daddy put his on the kitchen table sometimes after he had been shooting fours. I didn't know whether I would faint or cry or become invisible or explode, anything seemed more likely than that I would feel this chaos of strange love well up in my blood. I felt as if Daddy had shot me from ambush and that I was mortally wounded and that the gaping great bloody hole in my chest and heart was the dearest prick of pain and forgiveness and loss of hope that ever touched the purest part of man or child.

I said, "Daddy, I shot at you through the window. It was me."

He said, "You'll never guess who told me."

I said, "About me shooting at you?"

He said, "No, about the eunuchs."

I said, "Mavis Mitchum?"

He said, "Nope."

I said, "The midgets?"

He said, "No, of course not the midgets, that's silly."

I said, "I know who it was then. I know exactly who it was."

He was proud of me for guessing. He said, "He's a smart little bugger, ain't he?"

I said, "How does he do it, Daddy? Is it really Mr. O'Kelly who knows these things? Is it really the blind man?"

He looked surprised that I would say such a thing. He said, "Mr. O'Kelly?—that pore thing?" He said, "Mr. O'Kelly don't know much of nothing, Sugar. Pore Mr. O'Kelly wouldn't last the night, if he didn't have Joseph of Arimathea to wait on him hand and foot."

I said, "Did you talk to them—the eunuchs?"

He said, "Let's go outside, I'll introduce you."

I left Big G. B.'s side without really even a thought. I don't know what he felt, or what G. B. Junior felt or did, whether he moved onto the stool where I had been sitting and took the place he should have had all along, or whether he found a quarter and played the jukebox against everybody's wishes. I just don't know, didn't think to look, didn't think to ask, even later.

Daddy held the door and we went out into the lashing rain. Daddy said, "They are looking for St.-George-by-the-Lake, the little Episcopal chapel Dr. Hightower built out of the old Swiftown depot. We'll ride out and show them where it is."

I said, "Is it a baptizing this morning?"

He said, "The Barlow child."

The eunuch who was driving the van wore a short haircut and no mustache or sideburns. He rolled down his window and said, "I sure appreciate your help in locating the place, Mr. Mecklin. It's some kind of weather we're having this morning."

Daddy said, "This is my boy Sugar. Y'all just get behind us, we'll lead you out to the church."

The rain slacked up some, though it didn't quit yet. The turkey hunters—one or two of them—had already started out to their trucks. The woods were flooded, there would be no hunt today. Me and Daddy led the eunuchs out of town toward St. George, the old converted depot down by Roebuck Lake.

THE SEARS AND ROEBUCK
CATALOG GAME

I had known for a long time that my mother was not a happy woman. When I was a young child in Mississippi, the stories she read to me at bedtime were always tales of Wonderland—of little worlds into which one might escape through rabbit holes or looking glasses or magic wardrobes. The same was true of the games she and I played together.

My favorite game was to open a Sears and Roebuck catalog and to sit with my mother on the floor or in her lap in a chair and to point to each model on the page and to say, What does this one do?—where does this one live?—which one is her boyfriend?

My mother was wonderful at this game. She made up elaborate dossiers on each of the characters I asked her to invent. She found names and occupations and addresses and proper mates for each. Sears and Roebuck was a real world to me, with lakes and cities and operas and noisy streets and farmlands and neighborhoods.

There was even death. Mother shocked me when I was ten by reporting a suicide among the inhabitants of Sporting Goods. I loved and was terrified by the unpredictable drama and pain.

My father had no imagination. He disapproved of the game. It is more fair to say that he was baffled by it, as he was by all forms of imaginative invention. He did not forbid games or movies or books or Bible stories; he simply did not understand what use they could be to anyone. At night when my mother had finished saying my bedtime nursery rhymes to me, he would sometimes say to her, "Why do you do that?"

The summer I was fourteen I had occasion to think of the catalog game again.

I had taken a job working for my father on a painting site at the county high school. The local swimming pool was directly behind one wing of the schoolhouse, so while I should have been carrying ladders or washing brushes or wiping up paint drippings, I was usually hanging out the window watching the swimmers in the pool.

That's what I was doing one Friday afternoon, when I happened to see a child drowning. I don't know how I happened to see her. Even the lifeguard had not noticed yet. It was a gangly retarded girl with long arms and stringy hair plastered to her face.

I watched her rise up out of the water, far up, so that half her body showed above the surface, then she sank out of sight. Once more she came back up, and then she sank again.

By now the lifeguard was in the water and the other swimmers were boiling up onto the sides of the pool to get out of his way.

After a while the child's body was retrieved, slick and terrible.

We stopped work for the day. Nobody said anything, we just stopped and loaded the van and drove away.

That evening Father sat in his room in his overstuffed chair and drank glass after glass of whiskey until he slept. He was not grieving the death of the child. Death sparked no tragic thoughts for him, no memories, he drew no tragic conclusions. He felt the shock of its initial impact, and then he forgot about it.

The reason he was drinking had to do with my mother. He was preparing himself for whatever drama was certain to develop now that she knew of the death. Drama was the thing for my mother. When there was none she invented it. When one came along she milked it for its every effect.

My mother went into the guest bedroom—the room she called the guest bedroom, because she loved the sound of the phrase, which suggested to her the possibility of unexpected visitors, longterm guests, though actually it was her own room. It had her bobbypins on the dresser, her facial creams, a hairbrush, her underwear in a drawer. She closed the door.

Down the hall my father was drunk and snoring in his chair.

I went into my father's room and watched him snore. I opened the drawer of his bedside table, as I had many times when I was alone in the house. I took his pistol from the drawer and found the clip. I shoved the clip into the handle and shucked a cartridge into the chamber. I flicked the safety on and off, clickety-click. I unloaded the pistol again and put everything back where it belonged.

My mother was standing in the doorway of the bedroom. My insides leaped when I saw her there in her nightgown. She said, "You are your mother's child."

We walked together to her room, her arm around me, my arms stiff at my sides. We sat on the edge of her bed together. She told me she understood why I wanted to kill my father. She said, "It's natural. Every son wants his father to die."

I wanted to say, "I don't want him to die," but I knew this would disappoint her, would spoil the drama of her pronouncement.

She said, "Death is a beautiful thing. Death is the mother of beauty."

I said, "I guess so."

She said, "Do you love me?"

I said, "Yes."

She said, "I love you, too."

She said, "How much do you love me?"

I wished I was in my father's room watching him snore.

She smiled when I didn't answer. It was a very cute smile. She seemed younger than she was. Younger than me, even. She said, "If I asked you to—oh, let me see now, what could I ask my young man to do for me?—if I asked you to, well, to *kill me*"—here she laughed a silvery little-girl laugh with silvery bright eyes—"if I asked you to do that, honey, would you do it?"

I was terrified and sick. I thought I might vomit. And yet in a way I thought she might be joking with me, that there was a grownup joke here that I didn't understand. I said nothing, I couldn't speak.

She looked at me and suddenly her face changed. Her voice changed.

She said, "I just want you to know, there is no reason to be ashamed of discussing the subject of death. Death is a natural part of the whole-life process."

She propped two pillows against the headboard and leaned against them. She motioned for me to sit beside her, but I stayed where I was, on the edge of the bed.

She said, "Do you want to talk about the drowning?"

I couldn't answer.

She said, "After an incident of this kind, the healthiest thing in the world is to talk about it. I'm interested in your feelings about death."

I said, "I saw her drowning before anybody else. Before the lifeguard."

She told me the strangest story. It was exactly like a story she might make up about the Sears and Roebuck people, except that it was about herself; there was no catalog. She told me she was born in Saskatchewan. (Remember that not a word of this is true. She was born in Mississippi and had lived nowhere else in her life.) She said that her family had lived in a four-room fifth-floor walkup with cold Canadian winds whistling through the chinks in the thin walls. "Cold Canadian winds," she actually said. "The thin walls."

I wanted to call out to my father, but I knew he was too drunk to wake up. I knew I could not call out anyway, because it would say the truth to her, it would say, "You are insane, you are ruining my life." I wanted to protect her from that embarrassment.

She said that her mother had earned a pitiful living for their entire family by beading bags for rich women. (Where on earth did she come up with occupations for her characters? One of her catalog people was a crowd-estimator. Another was a pigeon-trainer.) "My mother," she went on, tearful, "sat huddled over her georgette-stretched beading frame, her fingers feeding beads and thread to her crochet needle like lightning." I was torn between the wonderful melodrama of the story and the dangerous madness of it. "My cruel Canadian father," she said (her father was a man from Tennessee, with a white mustache and stooped shoulders and a brace on one leg) "my cruel father spent every penny of my mother's hard-earned money on a mahogany gold-handled walking cane and sunglasses and pointy-toed shoes made of kangaroo skin."

She stopped suddenly and swung her legs off the bed and stood up. She sent me from the room and closed the door hard behind me, as if she were annoyed.

I was relieved to be set free. I got undressed in my room upstairs and slipped into bed and lay still. I thought of the things she said: the beaded bags, the kangaroo skin shoes.

I never mentioned this incident to my father. I was afraid he would find out I had been playing with his pistol.

In many ways, despite my mother's lapse into madness, I remember this as the happiest summer of my life. There were quiet times and funny times. Mother sewed in the dining room on the portable Kenmore. Father went to work and came home smelling of paint and turpentine and whiskey. He fed the chickens in the backyard.

Mother redecorated the living room. It was not a big project, but not small either. The sofa was reupholstered, there were new pictures for the walls (one, I remember, was a bright poster with parrots). A white-painted wicker chair was brought in, the old rug was replaced. There was a tropical theme, I would say, with a couple of large ferns and hanging baskets.

Who knows what the decoration of this room meant to my mother. Something from a Bogart movie, a Graham Greene novel.

I continued to work (to loaf!) at the schoolhouse. I fetched and toted, I cleaned up paint drippings. I collected my weekly paycheck.

Though I worked six days a week, my time seemed my own. I swam in Roebuck Lake—a lake that, according to one of my mother's stories, was created by an earthquake and was "bottomless." I dived into it and brought up its stinking mud in my hand. I tasted whiskey for the first time, with two other boys at a dance. A girl named Alice Blessing let me take off her bra. The summer was golden and filled with new joys.

The schoolhouse job was nearly completed. Summer was almost over. One day late in August, my father sent me home from work early. Later he said he sent me to check on my mother, though I didn't know this at the time.

I walked into the living room and found Mother sitting naked in a wicker chair. I had not seen her naked since I was a small child.

She was holding a razorblade in the air above the veins of her left arm. She did not press the blade to her flesh, only held it and pretended to draw it along her arm. A pantomime of suicide. The skin was untouched.

When she was done, she placed the blade on the glass-topped table in front of her and slipped into a silk robe that lay across the arm of her chair.

She sat back and looked at me. It was a brazen look, without apology.

And then—this sounds as if it is a dream, but it is not—my mother picked up the razorblade again and put it to her left arm and opened an artery.

I couldn't move. The blood soaked her robe to the armpit. It spilled through the wicker. I watched my mother's face become the face of a child and then of an old woman and then a hag-witch, unrecognizable.

I saw all her life in her shattered face—the hidden tyranny of her father, her frightened acquiescent mother, a drunken husband she never loved, a child she never wanted—and at the same time a sad dream of dances with the governor's son on someone's cypress-shaded veranda, the wisteria and jonquils and lanterns and laughter and music.

I moved toward my mother, one step, another, until I had crossed the room. I stood in her slick blood and clamped her arm in my hands.

I pressed hard, with such a fierceness of anger and love that the near-lifeless arm rose up at the elbow as if it had life of its own.

I let go with one hand and stripped a shoelace from my shoe and brought it up as a tourniquet. I picked up a brass letter opener from the table beside her and slipped it into the tourniquet and twisted it like an airplane propeller. The shoestring bit into my mother's arm. I twisted and twisted until I thought the shoestring would break.

I held the tourniquet tight and did not faint.

My father came home and found us there, statue that we made together, pale as marble.

My mother lived longer than my father, it turned out. She is alive today, in Mississippi, where she is friend to a woman I once loved and was married to. My mother is an attentive grandmother to my children—two sons, whom I no longer see. She plays charades and board games with them on her porch and offers them Coca-Colas from her refrigerator. She makes shadow-shows for them on her bedroom wall at night. She is gray-haired and serene and funny.

She calls me on the phone occasionally and laughs that she is not much of a letter-writer.

The scars on my mother's forearm are pale and scarcely noticeable. Nobody seems to care what happened so long ago.

But the afternoon my mother opened her arm and was taken to the hospital, I believed my father would live forever and that the world would always be as manageable as it seemed then. I had saved my mother's life—there was a practical fact that could not be changed. It was the kind of simple, necessary thing that my father could understand and appreciate, and now I could appreciate it too. I could do it and then go on living, with no replays of the event in dreams, no additions or corrections, no added details, no conclusions about life. I was my father's son.

While Mother was still sick, we spent our days alone together doing man's work—the paint and the ladders. Afternoons, we spent beside Mother's hospital bed. We adjusted the IV bottles, we saw the stitches, we heard the doctor's suggestion that Mother go into therapy.

Nights we spent in the kitchen of our home. We boiled po-
tatoes, we floured and fried cubed steaks, we made milk-gravy
in the grease. It was a simple, manageable life. It required no
imagination.

Many years later, when I was grown and my mother had
learned to live her life, I would travel back to Mississippi to
wait out my father's last days. His liver was large and hard and
showed through his clothing. His eyes were as yellow as gold,
his face was swollen.

One afternoon of the visit, I took my eyes off him for a few
minutes and, sick as he was, he escaped from the house and,
with the last of his strength, crawled far back under the house
and died there in a corner, beneath the low waterpipes. I
crawled on my belly, back where his body lay, and tied a length
of rope around his feet and pulled out the jaundiced corpse
dressed in pajamas. A retarded woman named Mavis Mitchum, who lived next door, watched the whole operation
while sucking on the hem of her skirt.

At my father's funeral the minister said, "He brightened
many a corner." It was hard to know whether to laugh or cry.

But at our kitchen table those late nights when my mother's
life was so recently out of danger, we were alive and beautiful
together, two men in the fullness of our need and love. Each
night my father was fragrant with whiskey, and each night I
relinquished more of my heart to his care.

I joked with him, knowing how he would respond. "So Roebuck Lake has no bottom—is that the story?"

He said, "You'll never get me to believe it."

We laughed, without guilt, at my mother's expense.

I said, "I can dive down and bring up mud."

He said, "Well, there you are. No two ways about it."

He poured Aunt Jemimah syrup over the last of his cornbread. He was ripe and wonderful with alcohol.

I don't remember now, these many years later, who suggested that we play the Sears and Roebuck catalog game. I
must have suggested it. I must have wanted to tease him in
some way, by suggesting a thing so antithetical to his nature.
I must have thought it would make him laugh. Or maybe I
thought to dispel more of the influence of my mother's bad

magic, the strength of imagination that had brought her to madness and near death. The game must have been my idea.

And yet I think I remember that it was my father who wanted to play. I think I remember that he pushed back from the table, contented and tired from the day's work, happy with a stomachful of cornbread, and that when he had wiped his mouth on his napkin, he said to me, "You know what we ought to do? You know what might be fun, now that Mama's all better and coming home soon? We ought to play us a little game of Sears and Roebuck."

Anyway, I got the catalog and brought it to the kitchen table. We opened it at random and sat and stared into its pages and waited for the game to happen. It was not easy to do this without Mother.

We were awkward at first, embarrassed. We looked up at each other and laughed. We looked at the catalog again.

Nothing.

We were in Women's Clothing. There were models: one woman stood alone and looked off into the distance, as if she were expecting someone. The wind seemed to be blowing. I said, "Who is she waiting for?"

My father stared at her for a long time. He was serious. I could see the strain in his face. He was trying to read the mind of the model in the picture, trying to imagine what on earth she might be doing there.

My father had no experience in this. It was painful for him. Despite his efforts, he was drawing a blank. He began to breathe hard and to perspire.

I said, "We don't have to play."

He said, "She's . . ." But it would not come to him. Finally he said, "I don't know." There was defeat in his voice. He had lost the early confidence he had had when the game first began.

I said, "Let's try somebody else."

We turned a page or two. We found two women laughing, with their arms hooked together. One of them seemed to be inspecting the heel of her shoe. I said, "Are they sisters, maybe?"

Father was working hard. He wiped sweat off his upper lip

and stared. At last he shook his head, very slow, side to side. He said, "I just don't know."

We tried other models, in other sections of the catalog. One man with a thumb hooked in his jacket pocket—he was looking back over one shoulder. There were men in hunting clothes and camouflage and raingear. Women in winter coats or in their underwear.

They seemed false. Nobody seemed alive. There was no geography to read from their faces, which were poses for a camera.

At one point my father said, "Your mom would look nice in a coat like this."

My father and I were incapable of inventing a world together. We were too much at peace in the one we already shared. The best we could do was to shop for clothes for the woman we loved.

My father seemed resigned but disappointed that the game was over. We sat back in our chairs. The kitchen was warm from the oven, where we had made cornbread. The dishes were still on the table, the food was beginning to congeal on the plates. Father closed the catalog.

And then, as an afterthought, he opened it again. He turned to Women's Clothing and found the picture of the woman standing in the wind and looking into the distance.

He said, "I think I'm beginning to see."

What might a man see, sitting at a table with his son? I wonder what I might say to my own sons if they were near me. I might say, "She is looking into the past to see what went wrong." Or maybe, "She sees pitfalls to avoid, opportunities to embrace."

At the time I only felt a vague fear, a tearing loose of something I had imagined to be permanent.

My father said, "She sees me."

It was in this moment that my father's imagination was born.

The rest of his days he spent in misery. He remembered the war. Though he had never spoken of it before, now he told funny stories about it, touching stories. Over time he changed the stories, embellished them, emphasized their comedy, their pathos, he added characters and details. He remembered a woman he had met in Florida at the circus. Later he said she worked in the circus as a swordswallower and fire-eater. Another time he claimed to have been in love with her and to have asked her to marry him. He could weep real tears over this loss.

He became secretive. He hid peppermint candy in his sock drawer. He carried his pistol in his car. He bought a black suit of clothes with the words *Rock 'n' Roll Music* spelled out in sequins on the back. He kept it hidden in the back of his closet and never wore it in public. He learned to dance at the American Legion Building and I am almost certain he had an affair with a woman who worked there. He watched television day and night. He thought about his childhood. The Sears and Roebuck catalog had ruined my father's life.

Even at the kitchen table I knew it was ruined.

I said, "This game is not true. This is Mother's game."

It didn't matter. The damage was already done. I looked at my father through the eyes of the model in the picture and saw what she saw: the face of a yellow corpse beneath our house and in that face an emptiness too vast ever to be filled up or given meaning. I looked away, in fear of what else I might see.

THE FARMERS'
DAUGHTER

The columned home was not an outrage, not yet, or not still, not outrageous like Sutpen's Hundred, hewn and hacked into William Faulkner's fictional wilderness near Frenchman's Bend, Mississippi, by a band of wild and shirtless Negroes, not outrage but epitome, real but a year older than Sutpen's Hundred if that had been real, built in 1832 upon the banks of a river that a generation ago moved and left the home and its dozen Doric columns cut off from main roads save one, and it no main road any longer, first alternate than spur then no road at all, paved still but out of use. The Farmer mansion was epitome and apotheosis for Dixie Dawn Farmer of all that held her trapped in her sixteenth year in 1971, circumscribed within its walls, an image of her family. In the front yard Johnson grass grew as high as a man's head, up to the rotting veranda, where Barfoot played bugle, and in the back kudzu crawled where wisteria might have hung or lain before her father was eaten by the bear and the Confederate cavalry bugle fell into the possession of an ironic man. The house was crumbling but not yet and not still an outrage, for only sex or death produce that, not the soundless vacuum in which in an earlier time events transpired without sound, faded and vanished, or without much sound anyway, and left Dixie Dawn immobilized, impotent, helpless, fixed, until she could secrete herself among the pages of *Absalom, Absalom!* or *The Sound and the Fury* or the other Southern Gothic that filled her shelves and her mind in the high-ceilinged massive-windowed room which held her canopied bed. The legend, like the house, was a personal epitome, compendium, and apotheo-

sis—house, novels, rumor, imagination—legend but unarticu-
lated, like nothing else in history but partaking of the entire
spiritual history of the Farmer family, boiling, broiling, moil-
ing in her mind like a pack of dogs when the bear is at bay,
family legend, dreamed, imagined, insinuated, emblematized
in the library of the home, which shamed or redeemed itself
with a smell, an odor, not of death merely but also of the be-
ginnings of life, bloody but seminal—this part not imagined,
as most had to be, a real smell, stink, and one thing more: the
black hand of her ancient great-grandmother, a billion speckles of black, but seeming black in its entirety, black enough for
Dixie Dawn, great Aunt Sugar with the one black hand. There
were two things then that were not dreamed, smell and hand.
Three, if Barfoot's insinuations could be believed, her stepfather's. This was the miscast summer of her barren youth,
when what she knew and what was unknowable, mythic, leg-
endary, Gothic like the fiction she fed upon, were the same,
a summer when what was dreamed but undreamable was inseparable from what was true empirically, the same in her
mind inseparable, inexorably fixed in a kind of new truth of
its own. The stepfather, Barfoot, born Linden Barfoot, re-
named by the act of hyphenation Linden Barfoot-Farmer
when he married Dixie's mother (a great and silent woman,
Delta Dawn Farmer) until at last his surname became his first
and left him ironic, had said on the veranda swing with Dixie
under his arm and the bugle on his lap, "Honey, your Aunt
Sugar held no grudge against any bear. She was trying to
kill Uncle Billy." Aunt Sugar, in the rocker, almost smiling,
touched the black hand with the white and rocked gently in a
near-summer breeze. This—even this—in that near-summer
of her sixteenth year, was enough. Mythic flurries sprang from
her brain, alive and real to her, despite the unrelenting irony
of Barfoot's face: William Wordsworth Farmer, her real father,
a medical doctor, graduated from the Vanderbilt School of
Medicine and interned at the Ellisville Institution for the
Feeble Minded of Mississippi (to be near kin, Barfoot said), was
killed and eaten in the library of their home when Dixie Dawn
was still an infant. It must have been that way, she told herself,
when even Barfoot's irony was sufficient, when the slightest

word would have been enough to convince her. Killed and
eaten in the library of their home. Yes. That bear, the third-
generation progeny of another bear, long since dead, captured
as a cub in the Tallahonka flatwoods by Kimbrough Hightower
Farmer, William Wordsworth's grandfather, and given to his
son's wife (the black-handed old Aunt Sugar) as a wedding gift.
The bear, the gift of life, growing to maturity in the Farmer
library, knowing nothing of love save that of human hand, not
even, as Aunt Rosa Coldfield told Quentin, a parent's love, that
fond dear constant violation of privacy, that stultification of the
burgeoning incorrigible *I* which is the meed and due of all
mammalian meat, the bear, if Dixie Dawn was right, became,
like Dixie herself, all polymath love's androgynous advocate,
inhabiting as her den the Farmer library, conceiving and giving
birth among the Morris and Wedgewood chairs and ancient
loveseats and leather-bound volumes of Horace and Cicero.
Dixie Dawn pored over "Uncle Willy" and "Old Man" for another clue but found none. The bear's world would become her
own, the vague inference of some walking flesh and blood de-
sired by someone else even if only in a shadow realm of make-
believe, a shadowy emergence of sex and birth and death and
now all that and William Faulkner too, mixed up in her sixteen-
year-old mind in a dream of a former age in which all things
happened, in which a male bear, driven by the same lust as the
human animal, walked out of the woods in 1948, onto the
porch of her home (she still seven years unborn) and mounted
the resident second-generation bear (itself conceived in this
same room) and in friction's ravishing of the as yet male-
unfurrowed meat, met in the act of generation in the same
room with Uncle Billy Philly. The bear and her mate must
have left, must have abandoned the cub which was their progeny, offspring of glands and lust and yes love, even that, and
left that cub to grow to maturity alone, the cub which must
surely have eaten Dr. Farmer, her father. Uncle Billy would
have seen it all, if only he would tell. He would remember,
perhaps, that the bear had devoured William Wordsworth
(Uncle Billy sitting in audience at the conception of the bear
and the death of the man) and then have watched the bear
live at peace with herself and the rest of the family until some

symbolic day, Christmas Eve (that festive season) or New Year's Day of the following year, when Aunt Sugar Farmer, the grandmother, unsentimental, unspeaking (she had not spoken a word during the five years since her ninetieth birthday), Sugar the monolithic and silent progenitor of three generations of bears, for she had received the cub on her wedding day, took a rib-steak from the refrigerator and a loaded Confederate handgun from the gun case, walked into the library, and killed the bear in its tracks. Uncle Billy Philly must remember but would not tell that she stood in the french doors of the room, the steak in one hand, the gun in the other, two feet from the bear's face, no more than that, and said, "Open up, motherfucker," said this and never spoke again, and when the bear opened its grateful mouth, placed inside it not the steak but the pistol and blew out the animal's brains. The old firearm must have been overloaded, overprimed, must have blown to smithereens in her little hand, as ball and shrapnel dropped the beast in its tracks and that magnificent woman's hand and lower arm turned black with gunpowder. That was in a summer long ago. Now in this new summer, this season of a virgin's itching discontent, William Faulkner could help but must finally leave unscratched that stormy region of a young girl's flesh which dead pages cannot touch so well as the living meat.

Since that day only Billy Philly, and on cleaning days his wife, Sweet Sugar Farmer Philly, ever entered the library again, if Dixie Dawn's reasoning was correct.

Uncle Billy claimed "family" even less authoritatively than the bears, having married into the household through William Wordsworth's sister, Sweet Sugar Farmer, whereas two generations of bears were actually born in the house, yet (and this phenomenon observable empirically, daily, not reconstructed in a child's mind) he alone felt no hesitation about entering this room, selecting a book from the maple shelves, and reading for the entire day, as he had done every day of Dixie Dawn's sixteen years in the family home, and seven years before that.

Delta Dawn would not enter the library, not from stated conviction, belief, but intuition, as though she knew without saying that the nooky seat of the ancient chair in which her brother-in-law sat, which even when he left it to eat the black-eyed peas and cornbread and drink the icy buttermilk at the cherry table in the dining room, held invisible imprint of his absent thighs just as the very sun and moony constellations that looked down on him in the circumambient air in the stink, gave him sole proprietorship of room and seat and book and stink. And Barfoot did not enter either, did not because he worked, supported this household of self and wife and stepchild and Sugar and Billy and Sweet Sugar and the Philly daughter, Lovie Alice, and a maid one hundred fourteen years old (a big girl at the Surrender), who inhabited an upstairs bedroom and had to be waited on hand and foot, Brown Sugar Farmer, a Negress. He (Barfoot) worked eighteen hours a day, never entered the library (and could read neither Latin nor Greek) and acquired through the phenomenon of cohabitation a Confederate bugle and by the act of hyphenation a new name and a streak of irony. On another day, not in the veranda swing but sitting with his stepdaughter upon her tall four-poster bed, where Dixie Dawn lay aside *The Unvanquished* and listened, he (Barfoot) said, "Uncle Billy's prerogative in that room was gained through his presence at the conception and death of one of the bears." And she believed. It made sense to Dixie Dawn. He kissed the child and loved her like his own daughter and they promised by their love, not with words but with a suspiration of twinning souls, to bear the weight of the murmurous myriad voices of the past. On the veranda after work each day he played bugle calls and he bought Dixie the complete works of William Faulkner, but he did not enter the library. "Why don't you, Barfoot?" she asked him from the bed. "Why don't you ever go in there?" and his reply, "Stinks too bad, honey."

The Phillys had come to the home nearly twenty-three years earlier to deliver Sweet Sugar of her first and only child, as was the custom of Mississippi families of quality, in the home of her brother, Dr. Farmer. Billy, like the fictional Eula Varner before him, was lazy, incorrigibly lazy, though not with the constant bustling cheerful idleness of a Will Varner (though he was cheerful enough, and always rested), not that exactly, but, like Eula, had honed and shaped his sloth until it became an actual force, impregnable. Barfoot claimed to like the man and confided to his stepdaughter that Billy Philly was an artist, a creator of a new thing, a *dichter,* and that his creation was a laziness so profound that in a good light it could actually be seen sitting in the chair beside him. Dixie Dawn knew that in the dozen or so years of her memory Uncle Billy Philly, except for the normal movements of dressing and cleaning himself, had never lifted a hand that did not carry food to his mouth or a book to his lap (though he was trim and handsome a man as a young Colonel Sartoris), and she felt that given the choice between food and the written word he might first have abrogated the right to food. He read all day in the family library. He and Sweet Sugar, more than twenty years earlier, arrived at this house, she the protuberant female flesh bursting with ripeness, suggesting by her appearance some ancient but corrupted symbology out of the old Dionysiac times—honey in sunlight and bursting grapes—he, dressed in a white double-breasted Panama suit purchased from a traveling man in Itta Bena, Mississippi, the two of them arrived with bag and baggage and imminent baby, took up residence and made not a move to leave, and Billy made himself comfortable. Unlike her husband Sweet Sugar worked constantly. If the story of the bear were true, as indeed it must have been (as Dixie Dawn reasoned), if the outrage on both house and mammalian flesh had occurred, as in these latter tamer days of Dixie Dawn it did not, Sweet Sugar's main primary occupation until the death of the bear must have been cleaning the library where it lived. "Barfoot," Dixie said on the way to church in the Plymouth, the bugle on the seat between them (only they of the household were interested in religion, and they attended church regularly), "why did everything happen in the past?" and he had said that this was only a lull, that things would pick up if they were patient, and she: "Is that why Sweet Sugar works so hard? Getting ready for—something?" She had wanted to say, "Getting ready for another bear?" but that would have violated the mute silent pact between them, a tacit agreement that she would never speak directly of the thing itself but would wait for clues and, if she were patient, Barfoot would provide one. Barfoot drove on, as Dixie Dawn lay her soft face upon his fatherly shoulder, and he finally said, "When the bear was called to her reward, Sweet Sugar's loss was greatest." The word was out again, bear, bear, bear, a four-letter word, delicious and frightening, but out in the open. Would Barfoot's irony twice extend so far? Or was not this another clue? "How come?" she asked. "Because," he said, "nothing short of a full-grown bear, living, eating, mating, sleeping, and shitting in the library of a residence could satisfy her insatiable rage for work." She recognized this as irony, like the bugle calls, but it still might hold some solid evidence. Sweet Sugar, in these drab, ungolden days of the present, in which, as Dixie Dawn believed, nothing of importance ever happened, was reduced to regular cleaning duties, and especially to ironing and reironing clothing for the entire household, including that of the nonambulatory maid, Brown Sugar. She loved pleats. When all the cloth in the house was ironed, creased, sheets, suits, socks, anything vaguely ironable, she sprinkled them heavily with water and ironed them again, and as she did she muttered audibly to her grown daughter through clenched teeth, "Sweet Jesus. Sweet Jeeez-us, your daddy is a lazy man." Their daughter, Lovie Alice, only smiled and nodded like the southern lady that she was. "But I do love him so," said Sweet Sugar, her hair wet with sweat.

Billy Philly sat in the Wedgewood chair by the window of the library and read Cicero, or if he were feeling sportive, Catullus. He had no other occupation than this, and it relaxed him greatly.

Dixie Dawn, upon her canopied bed in her room upstairs, reading, rereading, perusing the initiation rites of Ike McCaslin, trying to find, locate some clue, some hint of an insight into her own condition, perceived in her mind's eye that faceless substitution for Ike's half-breed mentor, the high priest who would preside over her own initiation, but she could see no face, not even Barfoot's, and so lay "The Bear" aside and lost herself on the corncob of Popeye. In the room across the hall Aunt Sweet Sugar ironed clothes and muttered to her daughter of twenty-two years, Lovie Alice (whose age like that of Benji Compson, was calculated first in the units column and only then by the tens digit, who, as Barfoot said, had been two for twenty years), the sole fruit of the Phillys' original journey to the Farmer mansion, spoke of the burden she (Sweet Sugar) bore: "Sweet Jesus, Lovie Alice, you don't know the burden I bear."

Lovie Alice Philly, to her mother the most beautiful girl in Tallahonka County, deaf, mute, and deeply mentally retarded, dressed in pink taffeta, "listening" to her mother's loving complaints, nodded her head in agreement with the casual grace of a Mississippi Miss America, or so it must have seemed to her mother, though Lovie Alice's jaw was inclined to fall slack and her eyes were dull blue.

Barfoot the ironic, who took his degree in Germanic philology at Tulane and worked days as a salesman of Kenmore sewing machines for Sears and Roebuck and nights in a rock and roll band in the Paradise Inn Supper Club, hours before he would come back home to bugle practice, Aunt Sugar with the one black hand, speechless, ancient, rocking in her chair, Brown Sugar, prostrate, sleeping, Delta Dawn the strong, anonymous, preparing meals for the entire family and special diets for the maid, Lovie Alice the beautiful, drooling, Sweet Sugar the cleanly, ironing, sweating, Dixie Dawn the nubile, reading Faulkner, listening, all of them who could, listening to the familiar sound from downstairs in the library: "Soo." Softly at first, and still softly, musically, "Soo. Sooooo." More loudly now, like a man calling pigs, "Soooooey, soooo-eeeee!" but still musically, a song for Sweet Sugar ironing on. "Soooo-eeeee! Soooey! Sooo-eeeeet!" She puts down the iron and starts down the stairs, Lovie Alice waving goodbye as well as she can. Across the hall Dixie Dawn rolls over and props on one elbow, listening still. "Sooo-eeeet Shu-gahh!" Dixie Dawn and all within earshot know this sound: it is Billy Philly calling for a kiss. Sweet Sugar is halfway down the stairs. "Sweeeet Sugahh!" he calls, she moving swiftly, reaching the bottom of the stairs, standing now in the library door, he sitting in a two-hundred-year-old chair by the window, a book on his lap, eyes closed, his face rested and happy, Sweet Sugar knowing what he wants since it is always the same, beads of sweat upon her brow and lip, hair plastered to her perfect neck. "You call me,

Billy?" she asks. Billy Philly opens his eyes, smiling, rested. "Kiss me, Sweet Sugar, *kiss* me!" he says, she still waiting. "Sweet Sugar, make me immortal with a kiss! *Da mi basia mille!*" She kisses him. "*L'amor che muove il sole e l'altre stell.*"

"Is that all, Billy?" she says.

"That's all, Sweet Sugar, that's all," picking up his book and reading softly to himself, she turning, walking from the room and up the stairs to her daughter who is struggling to place a goose-down pillow on the ironing board for her mother to work on.

"Sweet Jesus," says Sweet Sugar Farmer Philly.

Dixie Dawn, across the hall, thought briefly of Uncle Billy as he must have appeared, reading, as Dixie imagined, Vergil's *Eclogues*, not on this day but on the day a large male bear walked onto the front porch, through the door, down the hall, took the first door to the right, into the library, and mounted the resident second-generation bear, with whom Uncle Billy shared his waking hours. Had he (Billy Philly) in that hour of consummation, penetration, paroxysm, and catharsis of the warm and living mammal flesh been indifferent to the bellowing and the blood which punctuated Vergil's graceful phrase, or had he felt annoyance in the ammoniac density of the room and in the inexhaustible mammalian ineffable effulgence? She did not and could not know. She could only feel again the sense of loss in this latter day, when nothing of importance ever happened, as the past grew cloudier every day in the genetic amnesia and silence of her family. She heard her grandmother's chair creak and tip-toed through the hall to Aunt Sugar's open door and looked in. That ancient woman sat rocking almost imperceptibly, smiling an enigmatic smile, and rubbing the one black hand with the white. If only a bear would eat somebody today, thought Dixie Dawn, turning back. But there was no bear. Instead, she felt, she was doomed to continue forever, escaping into fiction from a houseful of lunatics with outrageous names. "I live," she said aloud to the walls of her room, "on the periphery of a bowdlerized Faulkner novel. All this place lacks is a dwarf." She picked up *The Hamlet* and read a lyrical chapter about a cow and a feeble-minded man named Snopes who loved it.

When the knock came at the door, Dixie Dawn (not yet undressed for bed, reading still another book) came down the stairs to answer it. Day was at its end, the mockingbird had already abrogated the songs of day for the nightsong, and the whippoorwills awake, singing with a drowsy moony fluting. Delta Dawn admitted their song and the rising moon and the stranger at the door before her daughter reached the bottom of the stair. He introduced himself, handed Delta Dawn a business card at which she glanced one time and lay on the hall table behind her. "Frank M. Carpenter," he said, smiling, weary.

"*M*," thought Dixie Dawn, stepping silently to the table to take the white card into her certain hand and lay unconsciously in its place the novel which she carried, read the card, and slip it unseen into what she called her underclothes, her brassiere, and feigning, adopting that abject secretiveness of childhood with a face poised halfway between cringe and welcome, querulous, she thought, "*M*, mmmmm," humming silently, "mmmmm, *M*—Moses, Frank Moses Carpenter."

"I am with a large drug firm in eastern Arkansas, Pfeester Pharmaceuticals," he was saying, "and . . ."

"Mmmmm," almost aloud, almost a moan, "*M, M, M*, mmmm, Motherfucker, Frank Motherfucker Carpenter," thought she, stopped, halted now in her tracks as surely as that mouthful of shrapnel must have stopped Aunt Sugar's bear.

"I am traveling to Atlanta to meet my wife and son . . ."

She stood transfixed, beautiful, aged merely sixteen but already beautiful, almost as bursting ripe as Sweet Sugar at twenty-five, if not in the fat grape and sweet wine of physical maturity, then more so in intensity of spirit and dreadful need and willing flesh and bone, at the bottom of the stair, her head full of the fluting of the whippoorwill and the mockingbird's song, and full of the magic Arkansas voice of Moses Motherfucker, which penetrated her soul. Her mood was strangely akin to that in which she lost herself in the band of wild Negroes on Sutpen's Hundred.

"I got off the main road, to admire your lovely Mississippi countryside," he lied generously, "and somehow onto this road before admitting to myself that I was hopelessly lost." He spoke with a humorous and mild air of self-deprecation and good-naturedness. "As a final humiliation," he laughed, "I inadvertently backed my car into a ditch a few miles from here as I was trying to turn around."

Deep in her mind she saw in a vision her own ghostly father, William Wordsworth Farmer, surrounded by three bears carrying Confederate bugles, and she heard her father say in an ironic voice profoundly familiar to her, "I am grieved, my good man, that we have no spare bed in this house to offer you. If, however, you are willing to consider some less comfortable arrangement, you may share a large double bed with one of these bears."

Her mother explained that there was no telephone in the house and that her husband, Barfoot, worked a late job three nights a week and would not be home until very late, but that Mr. Carpenter's car, she felt certain, would be safe until morning and that Mr. Carpenter was welcome to sleep on the sofa in the living room if he wished. "It's the front room," she said, failing to distinguish which of the front rooms she intended. Though Delta Dawn seemed to her daughter more loquacious than she had been for some time, this common-sense graciousness was typical of the woman, since it required no explanation of why Uncle Billy would not be able to help.

At this moment, in the instantaneous surrender of self, in a moment in which refusal might have been more gracious than acceptance, if less wise, Frank M. Carpenter chose wisdom and accepted this offer without fear, not even consciousness, that one instant later he would enter that blind chancy darkness called the future and would himself discover a need, dreadful yet delicious, and would penetrate by something of will and intensity an alien flesh with a need and will equally dreadful and more intense than his own. "Thank you," he said with relief. "I could not walk another mile," glancing as he spoke, without eagerness or abjectness but with something of momentary innocence into the brightening smile of the young woman at the foot of the stair.

"Won't you come in, sir," said Dixie Dawn, "you are most welcome here," spritely Aphrodite with milky skin and honey hair, turning on her heel and fairly dancing up to her room, listening deep in her blood to a song that she did not know was also sung in the weary but willing flesh and bone of Frank M. Carpenter, the song of all mammalian flesh, to Dixie Dawn the song of a bear in heat, listening and knowing that all life had not been lived in the past. *The Mansion* lay face down on the hall table.

In the middle of the night, the house, dark as any forest, taking on a new outrage, that of the girl, Dixie Dawn, an outrageous bravado, seemed to the girl to breathe with her in the despairing conviction that Barfoot had been right, that the lull was over, and that life could and would be lived again. She left the sheets which had held her virginal and vulnerable, possessing now a new conviction of her own invulnerability, irresistibility, believing that she, moving like a panther into the moonlight and down the uncreaking stair, had a soul as intrepid as that of her ancient great-grandmother who took arms against a bear, maimed herself and slayed, despairingly, the soulless creature who was the outrageous soul of this house. The past had died with the bear, and present and future were until this moment hopelessly emasculated and made impotent by its potent memory. When she reached the living room there was no sign of Frank M. Carpenter. The couch was empty. Sniffing the delicious air, puzzled, like a demon bear, teeming in her own fallow womanflesh, inhaling the stink of that other room on the front of the house, she turned toward it, the library, where fornication and a blackened pistol hand had been replaced by the dark impotent shape of Uncle Billy's chair in the cold dark light of the luminous moon in the corner by a window. On the Victorian loveseat lay the darkened figure of Frank M. Carpenter in his underwear. "He got the wrong room," she thought. Then, kneeling beside him, wetting her lips, thinking, whispering, "No, he got the right one," breathing deeply, almost silently, her hot breath on his sleeping face. She kissed him, not greedily, not at first, not outrageously, not yet, now merely tasting his lips, not devouring them. He stirred. "Open up, motherfucker," she whispered aloud. He woke, slowly at first, then with a start. "What the hell," he said. "What . . . Oh." He breathed more easily. "Miss Farmer. Dixie, isn't it? You gave me a little scare. Is anything wrong?"

"Go down, Moses," she said.

In the sleepy mesmeric senselessness of this stinking room with its leather books and Wedgewood chairs and crystal tapestry, Frank M. Carpenter came immediately alive to sex and fear and imminent outrage, seeming to Dixie Dawn to try to sit up without moving his body, searching the room without moving his reclined head, seeking wildly his clothes. She breathed life into his face. "Look," he said, fearful, exasperated beyond all normal endurance but already beginning to feel a power rise up in him, erect, in his body but not his voice, slithering closer to his pants. "Is this some kind of joke?"

Scuttling into respectability like a jackal into a woodpile, she thought, until she saw that he did not want the pants but only wanted to want them. "Yes," she said, "a dirty joke. Like my life in this house. You are a traveling salesman, and I am the farmer's daughter. Get it?" He would have gone by now, cried out, she thought, if he did not want it, glorying in her own potency and his accessibility.

"Farmer's . . ." he said, confused, bewildered at her and at himself. "Oh. Ha-ha. Yes. Farmers'. Ha-ha." She stopped his hand from reaching across to the chair on which his pants lay. "Ha-ha-ha," he tried again, convincing no one, least of all himself. Then with an attempt at greater gravity, hoping that in her innocence she would be convinced and that because she was so would he. "Now, Dixie, if I may call you that. I have had a very long long day, and though I enjoy a good joke, even one on myself, I . . ." His voice was trembling. "And though you must know that I find you—attractive—beautiful, in fact—I really do need to get some rest before tomorrow. Why don't you . . ."

"Open up, motherfucker."

He sat up, frightened of her and of himself, remembering that fornication's rewards, even with this young woman, victim until now of a hard celibacy which made importunate the blood of a young man, even with her a denial of the sadder task of his original journey, of a heritage more corrupt even than that emblematized in this, yes, outrageous house, and never sufficient, she breathing harder, kissing his mouth and face, he receiving her kisses, returning them. "Dixie," he said, with no conviction, "Dixie, darling, life is not a dirty joke. I refuse to accept that."

Dixie Dawn was Caddy Compson as she kissed his trembling lips.

"And I am not even strictly a traveling salesman. I am a kind of salesman, that's true enough, but I do not *travel* in the sense that you mean. So your little analogy . . ."

She was Lion the yellow dog and Frank M. Carpenter was Old Ben the great bear. She growled and struck his throat with kisses.

"I am traveling," he said, irrelevantly, mindlessly, not yet penetrating but already committed to the act of fornication, speaking in truth's own desperation, words that were at once explanation, exoneration, expiation, and outrage, "only in the sense that I am going from one place to another. I am going to Atlanta to pick up my wife and children who are at a hospital there." Frank M. Carpenter was completely naked, and Dixie Dawn was howling like a wolf. "Ooooo!" her howls piercing the night air and the ears of her almost cerebral Don Juan. She was Nancy in "That Evenin Sun," howling over a piece of blood meat to Jesus her husband who lay in his murderous ditch. He was in her now—or rather she was around him—straddling his lap and churning her slow and violent thighs.

"My older son," Frank M. Carpenter barely heard himself say, "is being treated in Grady Memorial Hospital." Then with the little voice that he had left, as he had surrendered his flesh like a sword, he relinquished his life to her care in confession: "My son is a dwarf."

For Dixie Dawn Farmer all motion stopped. All sound and breathing. The moon's rotation. The earth. All heartbeats ceased. "Soo," she said quietly, and their hips and the world began to turn again, as slowly as her voice was quiet. "Sooo!" she said, more loudly, their hips moving faster. A light came on upstairs. "Soooo! Soo, sooey, sooey!" Faster and faster. Blood and screams. "SOOEY!"

The top of the stairs creaked under the weight of a foot.

Faster and faster. Dixie Dawn was Aunt-Sugar-with-the-One-Black-Hand and Jesus-in-the-Ditch. She was Sweet Jesus Farmer, a black dwarf with a white hand. "SOOO-EEEEET!" she said. Violence, blood, destruction. Faster and faster. "SWEEEET JEEEZ-US!" she said.

Sweet Sugar Farmer Philly stood sleepily in the moonlit doorway of the library, and as she entered the room a bugle on the veranda sounded the Confederate *Charge!* Barfoot was home. *Charge! Charge! Charge!*

"Great God Almighty," said Frank M. Carpenter.

"You call me?" said Sweet Sugar Farmer Philly, and yawned.

The charge ended and Barfoot went straight into *Reveille* in earnest. You can't get it up you can't get it up you can't get it up this morn-ing.

Billy Philly turned from his moonlit chair in the corner of the library, a book resting comfortably on his lap. "No, Sweet Sugar," he said, very peaceful. "But kiss me anyway, Sweet Sugar, *kiss* me."

She walked across the room to the bugle's blare and kissed Billy Philly on the mouth. "Is that all, Billy?"

"That's all, Sweet Sugar, that's all. Go on to bed now."

Reveille finished and *Mess Call* began. Soupy soupy soupy.

Sweet Sugar yawned again and left the room.

Dixie Dawn waited until *Taps* was played, said good night to Mr. Carpenter and Uncle Billy. "Good night, honey," said Billy Philly. Mr. Carpenter said nothing.

Sweet Sugar was back upstairs in her room, where her gracious daughter, Lovie Alice, was awake, smiling a sleepy greeting and good night. Across the hall old Aunt Sugar continued rocking the night through in her high-backed cherry rocker and lay her white hand gently on her black one. Brown Sugar and Delta Dawn were in bed asleep. Day is done, gone the sun, God is nigh, said the bugle, as Barfoot finished up for the evening and then helped Mr. Carpenter get his car out of the ditch.

WILD DOG

When the first dog appeared out of the cane, the farmer was dozing with his back to a tree. The dog stretched its neck and put its nose into the wind, which was in the farmer's favor. The farmer shifted the rifle and released the safety.

Another dog stepped from the brake and stood with its fur riffling in the wind. Then others came out, younger dogs some of them, frisky and nervous. They prowled and pranced on the edge of the pasture.

The moon was high and white. The dogs grew calmer and began to bunch up. They scratched at fleas, licked a paw.

The rifle began. Brass casings leaped from it and brushed the farmer's cheek as he fired. Two dogs did not get up. The others scrambled, frantic, soundless, trying to become invisible in the moonlight, not even howling, not even those the bullets hit. He had to aim at each target.

Four were dead. Two others lay wounded, with their clear eyes open. He put the rifle to each head in its turn and closed the eyes. About a quarter of the pack. Not bad. Not bad shooting.

His shoes were bloody, and his hands, from dragging the dogs to a ravine. To keep Sally from seeing, he didn't turn on the water at the spigot. He dropped the bucket to the bottom of the cistern and drew it back, brimming, on the pulley. The water was ice cold on his hands and feet.

With her hands Sally smoothed flat the invisible wrinkles of a comforter and turned back the covers of the bed.

The ribbon at the throat of her gown was untied. She said, It's not just me, is it? I mean, I wish you would tell me if it is.

He said, No, I'm no farmer. It was a mistake. We've said this.

Still, she said, I feel, you know, guilty.

He said, We both tried. It just couldn't be done.

Later, in bed, she was silent. He thought she was asleep.

Then she said, Did you do it?

Do what?

You know.

I got six of them.

That was all for a while. This time he was almost asleep.

She said, I know they are dangerous. I know that.

All right.

Maybe rabies.

Yes, it's necessary.

She said, I love you.

He said, I love you.

She said, I'm still afraid you hold this against me. You worked so hard.

He said, No, of course not. It's necessary. We have to move back.

She said, In a way we are lucky.

He said, That's true. We're lucky.

Her voice was growing sleepy-sounding, and he knew it was almost over, for today anyway.

She said, Did they die right away? I mean, did they suffer?

He said, It was very quick. Don't think about it.

Do you ever think they are beautiful?

Don't think about this, Sally, if it upsets you.

Again the next night he was asleep in the pasture with the rifle across his lap. He dreamed an old man and woman in a car stopped beside him and asked directions.

The farmer woke. He could smell chimneysmoke from the house. There were no dogs tonight. He heard a goat bleat, a doe that had gotten its horns stuck in a square of fence wire, where it had tried to reach a clump of grass on the other side. He walked to it and released it and watched it bound away from him, the little tail writing curlicues in the moonlight.

Above him, on the mill road toward his house, clear as day, he saw a dog, a single. He could almost wonder whether this were another dream, an apparition, it seemed so strange to him. He did not reach for the rifle, which he had leaned against the fence. He watched the dog.

It moved as if through liquid, flowing along the road above him, following the narrow road through the moonlight like a magic thing, and then it was gone.

The farmer knew already, though. It was a bitch, slender and long-legged and big in the belly. He knew where it was going.

He took the rifle and ran, clumsy and stumbling. He crossed the fence so he could see past the little orchard, but he didn't see her.

The white smoke from his chimney was visible, and the night was bright—but she was gone. She had found the house already, was already under it. He knew she would have her pups there. Wild dogs beneath his house.

Onto his plate, beside the sausage and bread, Sally spooned brown applesauce. He ate without speaking.

She said, Will you kill it?

He said, Yes.

He remembered their first year here, four years ago. Sally had bought a quilt at a roadside stand. An old-fashioned design was stitched into it for decoration, a double muscadine. At the time it had not seemed a self-conscious thing to do. The quilt had seemed a necessary purchase for a proper farmer and his wife.

He said, Remember that quilt you bought? He almost said that quilt you made. The one with the grapes. Could we sleep under that quilt tonight?

She said, Remember?—it's already packed. You said maybe we could hang it on the empty wall near the staircase.

He didn't answer.

The apartment, she said. In the city. Then she said, I could get it out. I think I know which box.

It was colder tonight, he thought. The new owners would have to take care of the apples when they were ready. The young goats would have to be cared for—the billys would have to be castrated.

Sally found the right quilt and put it on the bed, but when

they got under it they were too warm and had to push it back. They propped up on their pillows in the dark and let their legs touch down their whole length.

She said, Can the new owners take care of it?

He knew what she meant. The wild dog. He said, It's no trouble. I'll do it in the morning.

Some time passed. He wasn't so sure he would do it in the morning. Something changed when he admitted he was not a farmer.

She said, Do you enjoy killing them?

It was her neutral tone. He would remain neutral as well.

He said, Farmers kill wild dogs. It's just the way it is.

She said, You said yourself you're no farmer.

Now they were close to the brink, so they stopped.

Later she pulled up her nightgown and he entered her. He felt her arms tighten around him and she felt his breath on her neck and ear. Soon it was over and both of them wanted sleep.

She said, I love you.

He said, I love you.

She was snoring lightly, and he was still awake. From beneath the house he heard a quiet yip-yip-yip from the bitch, and then that was over. He slept knowing the wild dog was already licking the wet dark eyeless shapes to life and form.

Before Sally woke up he left the house with the rifle and squatted at the trapdoor in the foundation of the house. He got on his hands and knees and then flat on his belly and began to pull himself along beneath the floorboards of the house and the network of waterpipes that lined them. He dragged himself forward a few inches at a time, then reached back for the rifle and pulled it to his side and started again. His legs cramped, and his neck and back.

The underside of the house was dark, but he found the dog. Despite the danger, he moved very close. The dog's breath was warm on his face, and it smelled of afterbirth. He wondered what strangeness the dog might smell in him.

He had not known he was going to do this. He touched the dog on its side, though he could scarcely see it and did not know whether his touch might provoke an attack. He knew this must be the first time the dog had ever been touched by a human hand. The fur was matted with beggars' lice and cockleburs. She did not flinch. He found her lean front leg and shoulder, and then he found the first pup at her side.

One, he counted aloud.

He removed each pup from its sucking, and allowed each to return.

There were seven.

His hand returned to the rifle. The dog's head was still raised and the calm breath still on the farmer's face. He held the rifle to the dog's head and did not release the safety. He would tell Sally there were seven.

The days passed and grew colder. More red and yellow dyed the skins of the apples. Slow rain changed the leaves to a dark shade of green. There were good crisp days of sunshine, and acorns beneath his feet.

The farmer split a fifty-pound sack of dogfood and placed it by the trapdoor of the house. Mornings some of the food would be gone, so he knew the she-dog was eating, though he never saw her eat.

Nights, by the pond, he sat with his back to the big cottonwood and watched for wild dogs. The nights were clear, and he loved the solitude of the fields and the constellations above him.

A few times he got a shot at a single or a pair, but the pack was gone, had moved on. Seven miles away, near the river, a man lost a colt, so the dogs were heading west.

The she-dog stayed away from the house and nursed the pups at a safe distance in the pasture. The bag of dogfood continued to diminish, so the farmer knew she was eating at night.

Preparations for the move back into the city continued. The rugs were rolled up, the curtains were taken to the cleaners.

In the kitchen one day he looked at the boxes and the clutter and the handful of dishes they were still using and he said, I should have killed the bitch and the pups. I'm so mixed up.

She said, I tried to love it here.

He said, It's not your fault. It's nobody's fault.

The pups were everywhere now, all over the yard and porch and pastures. They were big-footed and clear-eyed, clumsy and domesticated-acting. Each had a name now, and each had a collar and a tiny white flea collar. Each wore a silvery vaccination tag.

The she-dog did not come near the house, except once each night to eat in secret. She fed the pups their meal of milk far out by the pond.

It was the farmer who first brought one of the pups into the house.

She said, Do you think we should?

He said, I guess not.

She said, We really don't know what will happen—I mean, what we'll do with them . . .

He agreed that she was right, but he brought them in anyway. One at a time, evenings. He watched them play on the rug. He held them in his lap and scratched their ears with his finger. The she-dog moved closer to the house when the pups were inside, but still she kept her distance.

Sally wouldn't touch the pups. She wouldn't sit in the same room with them when they were in the house.

She said, It doesn't seem right.

He said, Why are you so cold?

She said, I'm not cold. Stop accusing me of being cold.

He said, You are cold.

She said, What are you going to do about these dogs? That's what we're fighting about.

The farmer said, We're not fighting about the dogs.

She said, It's horrible, it's perverse.

She was crying now.

He held her and tried to make her stop.

He said, It's nobody's fault. I'm no farmer.

She said, Let's go today. Let's leave everything behind and just go away this minute.

He said, I don't think I can start over again. We've started over so many times.

She said, I love you. She said, Maybe I don't love you. Maybe I just say that so you'll say you love me.

He was still holding her, with his face in her hair. He said, I'll take care of the dogs. I won't bring them inside again.

She said, I hate this goddamn farm.

He released her and walked away from her. He said, Stop punishing me, will you. Will you just stop? I know you hate the goddamn farm, so just stop saying it, all right? Jesus.

She said, I love you. She said, Maybe I don't. I don't know. Jesus, oh Jesus.

He didn't bring the dogs back in the house, but he didn't shoot them either. He stopped feeding them. When the last of the dogfood was gone, he did not buy a new bag. He thought they would go away, try to find the pack again. The she-dog would have the instinct, he thought. When she got hungry enough, she would take the pups and locate the pack. That's what he hoped.

When the food was gone, the pups were frisky and confused for a day. In two more days they still had not eaten. They were frantic. They had been weaned but they tried to suck at the she-dog. She snapped at them and kept them away from her. When one of the pups insisted, she took its face in her mouth and shook it and blinded the pup in one eye. She would not let them touch her.

In a week they were more frantic. In another week they were mad with hunger. They howled with pain. They scratched at the doors, back and front. The farmer and his wife felt like prisoners. The dogs' ribs stuck out. They were gaunt and horrible and did not resemble the dogs they had been.

The she-dog had been hungry before. She didn't care. She liked hunger as much as she liked food. Her eyes were crazy and resigned and looked like shattered glass, there was so much pain in them. Her fur fell out and her legs became stiff and painful to walk upon. She could have gone and hunted, but she didn't want to. She was arrogant, she was a judgment on the farmer and his wife.

They watched the dogs from their kitchen window. The pups were wretched and terrible. They lay in the pasture and ate grass. They wandered through the fields and scratched at the clay on the ditchbank and ate bark from the trees. They put their muzzles into antbeds and lapped up their own urine. They had no instinct for survival.

The farmer and his wife closed the shades against the sight of the miserable dogs. The farmer and his wife stood in their kitchen and sometimes they held each other and asked each other what to do.

The farmer said, They are wild dogs. Why don't they chase rabbits, or mice? Why don't they attack one of the goats?

The farmer's wife said, Shoot them. Get the rifle and kill them. I can't stand this.

At night the farmer and his wife slept, or tried to sleep. They decided to make love and then they changed their minds and did not. They lay naked without touching and listened to the pups whining at the doors. This happened many nights.

The pups changed more and more in appearance. Some of them were almost hairless now. Their bottom teeth showed above the gums, and the gums were discolored and gray.

The farmer's wife said, I'm going to feed them.

The farmer said, Yes, all right, let's do it, let's feed them.

They did nothing. They didn't kill them and they didn't help them live. Somehow the dogs' lives had gotten out of control, out of their hands.

So the farmer and his wife did nothing. They cleaned the oven and mended a board in the floor and swept cobwebs from the ceiling. They wrapped the last of the china in newspaper and packed it into boxes.

They tried not to listen to the voices of the starving dogs. And then they noticed that the dogs were not making noise any longer. The pups became old-looking and resigned and sickly. They lay in the yard and made no movement to look for food. There were other farmers, not a mile away, other houses, but the dogs did not try to find them. They did not search through the garbage. They became silent and almost sweet in their contentment with starvation. Their faces changed shape. Their hipbones were prominent. They lost their identities and could not be recognized by sight, and the names they had been given became pointless and irrelevant.

In the goatshed the alfalfa was as sweet as apples. The floor was fragrant with sawdust.

The she-dog was quietest of all. The farmer and his wife watched her and feared her. They were not sure why.

At first they said it was because they were afraid she would attack them. She's wild, they said. A few months ago she was part of a vicious pack. She was killing livestock. She could kill us.

The farmer's wife said, Let's not take a chance. Kill her first. She's dangerous.

The farmer said, I know I should.

The farmer's wife said, Do it then. Why don't you do it?

The farmer said, I will. I really will.

One of the pups died of starvation.

It helped. It was a release of sorts.

The farmer took the rifle from the closet and loaded the magazine and walked into the pasture and killed five of the others.

They were easy to find, and killing them was easy to do. The farmer wondered why he had allowed the punishment to go on so long.

The seventh pup he could not find. He looked in the goat-shed and under the house and in the woods and cane. The seventh dog was missing.

He said to his wife, I can't find it.

She said, Did you bury the others?

He said, I threw them into the ravine.

She said, I wish you could find it.

The moving company would come in one week exactly and they would move away from the farm forever.

The farmer said, I'll look for it tomorrow.

Sally said, Have you noticed the smell?—you can smell the she-dog all the way out in pasture.

The farmer said, I'll do her tomorrow too. Not today. I can't do her today.

The farmer and his wife were naked in bed. They did not allow their bodies to touch.

She said, Tomorrow, then.

He said, Yes, tomorrow.

She said, I love you.

He said, I love you.

She said, Why can't we stop saying this?

He said, I don't know.

She said, I never pictured myself as this person I've become.

They lay side by side for a long time.

He surprised his wife when he touched her, but she responded to his touch. She rolled over toward him and allowed him to hold her.

He wondered if she would say I love you again, and she did not.

She said, Today I couldn't find the broom. I didn't really need it, I just didn't know where it was, and it was all I could think about.

The farmer thought of the seventh pup and of the smelly old starving she-dog out in the darkness.

The bed the farmer and his wife lay in together felt as cool as the moist earth.

JOHN THOMAS
BIRD

Aunt Louise got Molly the date with J. T. It would do her good, her aunt said. And in the holiday sunshine of Gulfport, it didn't sound bad to Molly either.

But the minute she saw him she knew it was a mistake. He was beautiful. Spectacular, in fact. His skin was absolutely bronze and, still more astonishing, his body was bald. Not one hair that she could see on his arms or bare legs or the wide V of exposed chest. He was a magnificent golden statue of a man, blond and even blue-eyed, with strong limbs and a hard perfect waistline.

Molly wanted none of it. Or rather all, and so none. Handsome men scared Molly. Even ugly men were kind of scary if they were tall enough.

It was even worse to see him standing beside Aunt Louise waiting to be introduced. Together, in the cool breeze that swept off the Gulf and through the rattan blinds, Aunt Louise and the bronze young man looked like a Scotch advertisement in the *New Yorker*. Behind them, on a low table, stood a fish-tank, large and bubbling, its translucent occupants as serene as sails.

Molly's aunt was forty years old, the image of all that women diet to look like—tall and slim, her arms casually braceleted in thin gold rings. She wore tawny-gold bell-bottoms that she referred to only as "bells." A drawstring bunched up the waist so it almost but not quite covered the deep exposed navel beneath a silk halter, and her breasts were girlishly small. Molly folded her arms over her own large breasts to avoid a comparison.

"Molly," her aunt said sweetly, "this is John Thomas Bird—J. T." She was holding his hand and reaching out toward Molly to hold hers as well, smiling.

"Hi," Molly said, and allowed herself to be pulled closer than felt comfortable. She unfolded her arms unwillingly. Shit oh shit oh shit. Up close he looked even better. Why had she said Hi? Like a goddamn schoolgirl. "Hello," she corrected herself, grinning enormously for no reason that she could think of.

"Whatchasay there," J. T. said. The skin near his eyes twitched in what may have been a friendly way.

Aunt Louise was happy. She released Molly and put her arm around J. T.'s waist and pulled him along to a loveseat covered in a brocade of royal blue flowers. She told Molly, who trailed behind, that J. T. was second-baseman for the Air Force Base Special Services team.

J. T. ground a silent fist into an imaginary mitt.

They met at the Officers' Club, Aunt Louise said, where Uncle Walter still had base privileges, though Walter was, of course, retired, whereas "our Mr. Lieutenant Bird," she said, and squeezed his hand, was just beginning his career.

Aunt Louise laughed gaily at this thought, and Molly joined her, though as soon as she did she hated herself because J. T. did not laugh at all.

"We only danced the one time," Aunt Louise went on, "but I knew right that minute I would have to have him. For my little niece, of course. Who, by the way, isn't so little anymore." She laughed another silver laugh and Molly folded her arms again.

J. T. and Aunt Louise sat at almost the same instant on the loveseat. She snuggled comfortably in beside him and patted his naked knee in a confidential way. Even sitting so close on the little two-person seat, Aunt Louise could seem stretched out and luxurious. Molly took the seat nearest them, a Norwegian string chair. She had to remember to keep leaning back at all times to avoid having it snap shut on her like an oyster.

Having mastered the chair Molly suddenly realized it was her turn to speak. She had not been keeping up with the conversation, so she raced back to the information about the baseball team. "What position do you play?" she said. Goddamnit, second base, you dumbass, you know what position he plays. Oh let me out of this.

Aunt Louise looked puzzled at the question, but pleasant, and across the glass table between them, offered Molly the sherry again. When Molly saw it she knew how far off the mark her baseball question had been.

"Second base," J. T. said.

"Ah," Molly said. She had practically forgotten the question.

Aunt Louise had been following their little question and answer exchange as though it were a tennis match. Molly's "Ah," had gone into the net. Her aunt kept looking at her. Molly finally said, "What else do you do?"

J. T. said, "Stay in shape."

For a long ten seconds they sat in silence.

Standing abruptly, Aunt Louise said, "Now. You must please excuse me. I have stayed here too too long. You-all certainly don't need me, do you?" When there was no reply another wild silver-bells laugh leaped out. "So," she said. "You-all just talk and talk and talk without the likes of me around to . . ."

J. T. said, "Two of the most important things in life are a flat stomach and clear skin." He had apparently not noticed that Aunt Louise was speaking.

". . . interfere," Aunt Louise concluded, without much sound. For some reason she sank down onto the edge of the loveseat again.

I love you! Molly wanted to scream. Take me! Take me now, then kill me and my life will be complete. Forgive me for having big tits and a paunch, don't hate me for my freckles and my zits.

Instead, she said, "Does that include pregnancy and jock itch or just a fat gut and acne?" Why? she wanted to know. Why did she always say such things around men? Last year, when she was a senior in high school, a guy named Toby Blassingame found what he said was a sexual image in one of the assigned poems in English class. First thing after class she told him she masturbated. Why did she do things like that? Why did she make herself remember them? Toby Blassingame thought it was a joke. Everybody thought she was a great joker. She wondered whether all the jokers of the world were doomed to be virgins. And J. T. was right, she knew that. She longed for clear skin and a flat stomach, like Aunt Louise's. How could she be that beautiful woman's niece?

". . . interfere," Aunt Louise said again, but produced only slightly more sound than before. She didn't try again. She rose from the loveseat and left the room, still wearing her smile, which looked now like a lightbulb slowly burning out. Her slender figure faded out of their sight into the cypress-paneled recesses of the house.

Molly envied Aunt Louise's grace, her sophistication. But right now she was too distraught over her jock itch remark to think of her aunt. Where are all the ugly boys in this world? she asked herself. There was not one ugly boy on the entire Gulf of Mexico. Anywhere else you would see one or two.

And why did she always have to fall in love? She waited for J. T. to leave in disgust—she hoped for it in a way, longed for him to leave so she could go down to the beach alone, as she always did, and smoke marijuana until her mind was gone and maybe forget who she was.

But J. T. didn't move. He said, "Fish helps." Molly did not know what J. T. meant by this, but the phrase seemed to be offered as a form of masculine generosity, so she felt a little better.

She still felt fat and freckled and her pores felt larger than usual, but when she tried to beg off the date—or rather to let J. T. out of it—he never seemed to understand. She let the subject drop. She loved him. Why was she always "like a sister" to the boys she loved? J. T. hadn't said that yet, but he would.

Aunt Louise came back to say that she had made reservations for lunch and to suggest that an afternoon excursion boat "might be just lovely for you-all." Molly was surprised at the relief she felt when her aunt declined their invitation to go along with them.

Looking across an expanse of white sand by the Gulf, in what Molly hoped might be seen as a sophisticated way, she dared the scallops meuniere and tomatoes florentine to give her hives, and they did not. She got diarrhea instead. Not bad, and not from the scallops and tomatoes, but as always from anxiety.

It was made worse by her unexpected confession of it to J. T. "Sorry I was so long in the john," she said. "I got a slight dose of the trots."

Would this ever be over? She hoped J. T. could stand it a little longer.

In response, J. T. said, "Digestion is related to metabolism." Though he was looking directly at her, Molly could have sworn he was reading from a book, perhaps slightly above his grade level. "The physical condition of the entire trunk of the body," he continued. This made no sense at all, but Molly was grateful for his strange kindness. He said, "Ted Williams swung a weighted baseball bat one hundred times a day."

"And never had diarrhea?" Molly asked with interest.

There was a pause. J. T. said, "I really wouldn't know."

There was another pause. Molly said, "Isn't Ted Williams a male model for Sears now?"

J. T. said, "I don't think so."

Molly said, "Hm." During this pause a thought came to Molly like a voice. You are bored, the voice said. Not fashionably bored. For real.

Impossible, Molly retorted, and the voice went away.

J. T. said, "Mickey Mantle sells Houn' Dawg dog food, though."

Molly said, "Now who is Mr. Coffee?"

Later, as they were leaving the restaurant, J. T. said, "Swimming is a healthful watersport which is gaining rapidly in popularity." He fielded a sharp invisible grounder in the parking lot and fired it to first base.

Molly did not allow herself to wonder where J. T. learned to talk like this. She said, "Really? I'm a pretty good swimmer myself." What on earth did she mean by that? She was not a good swimmer. She was an adequate swimmer. A Red Cross Life Saving drop-out.

J. T. said, "Wanta go swimming? I heard of a good lake."
"Sure," Molly said. "Great." Oh shit.

In the woods beside the lake J. T. astonished Molly by taking
off every stitch of his clothing, right in front of her. She had
already put on her swimsuit, a tight green atrocity with a skirt.
After the restaurant they went back to Aunt Louise's to get it.

And now J. T. was naked. It wasn't sexual. Not even self-
conscious. It was the only way he ever exercised, he said; he
hoped she didn't mind. He always did warm-ups before he
swam.

Did she mind, she said. No, no of course not, she didn't, not
at all, go right ahead. Sure.

J. T. was the first man she had ever seen naked except in pictures. It is much better in the flesh, she decided. Entirely different. And much much better.

While Molly swatted mosquitoes under the moss-covered
trees, J. T. counted knee-bends in the nude. His eyes became
glassy, and three drops of sweat hung from his chin. His chest
glistened like waxed oak, and hair stuck to his neck.

There was no other hair on his entire body. A living breathing Nair commercial—the thought was inescapable.

After fifty knee-bends J. T. stopped in the down position,
his back perpendicular to the ground, his outstretched arms
perfectly parallel with it. He was beautiful.

She wanted to tell him so. To say, "You are beautiful," or "I
want you so much," anything to keep from saying "I love you."
She almost took off her own clothes, just to make him notice
her. She couldn't do it. He probably wouldn't notice anyway.
Why had she been in such a rush to get her own suit on? She
would look ridiculous taking it off now. It made no sense.
Next time she would wear every article of clothing she owned
so she could take it all off without embarrassment. Hell no,
that was a lie and she knew it. Nothing on earth could make
her expose those gargantuan jugs and freckled butt to J. T. or
anybody else as beautiful as he.

J. T. said nothing and did not look her way. His gaze re-
mained firm as he held the position twenty seconds. Then he

stood up and walked to a stump where he had laid out his swimsuit, jockstrap, and a clean white towel.

He dried each part of his body—carefully, thoroughly. Face, neck, arms, chest, legs. He used short rough strokes. Then he snapped the towel out to its full length and put it between his legs. He pulled it back and forth in a see-saw motion against his crotch.

It was too much for Molly. She could think of nothing to do with her hands, which suddenly felt fat. Nothing to talk about. She managed not to tell J. T. she loved him, so she didn't feel like a complete failure.

Then, without warning, she said, "I understand that masturbation promotes clear skin." Why in God's name had she said that? It was the worst thing she'd said all day. She might as well have told him she loved him. Her mind was gone.

And then she heard a voice say, "I've been masturbating for years and it hasn't helped a bit."

It was her own voice. My God, she thought. *I* said that. Why? I have now told two men, practically strangers, that I masturbate. One of them not even in a Lit class.

It didn't matter. J. T. seemed not to have heard. Placing the towel neatly on the stump, J. T. stepped into his jockstrap and red nylon swimsuit, bikini style, and if he noticed Molly there was no indication.

She followed him to the edge of the woods and sat beside him against a log. They looked at the water.

She said, "Seems kind of far across, doesn't it, Johnny?"

He may have nodded. She couldn't be sure.

The late afternoon sunlight broke into a timid dappling around him and over his shoulders as it filtered through the long gray beards of spanish moss in the trees above them.

If only she could leave now, get away and never see him again, it would have been a perfect afternoon and she could love him forever.

J. T. said, "John Thomas is a beautiful name."

Molly didn't know what to say, and nothing seemed required.

J. T. said, "It's such a strong name."

The head of a small turtle winked through the surface of the lake before them and stood still—so still that Molly thought

for a moment she had imagined it, that it was a stick instead.
The water blinked again and it was gone.

J. T. said, "Turtles are unusual." His tone and manner were
serious. He sighed. Molly would have said a philosophical sigh.
J. T. said, "Turtles are ashamed of their bodies."

There was nothing to say. Molly looked out at the lake and
knew that no woman on earth, no matter who she was, could
have thought of anything to say.

At last J. T. stood up and, without speaking, he walked out
into the water. Molly watched him as if in a dream. She
watched each step. The water seemed to sink beneath his foot
like a pillow. And then the other foot, the same. A million
speckles of rotted matter bubbled up around his legs in a
brown fog.

Molly followed him into the water, and her legs became
suddenly warm, too warm. The lake bottom was not sandy
but was soft with decay and then a little sticky when her foot
had sunk as far as it would go.

With each step leaves and brown stringy things that looked
like tiny root systems floated up from the bottom and brushed
against her legs.

J. T. seemed already to be a mile ahead of her, still wading.
She was trying to catch up when she saw him raise his arms
and dive forward and become a long green submarine beneath the surface of the lake. She dived behind him and felt
the water swallow her up warmly.

J. T. was a strong swimmer. He was outdistancing her
rapidly.

Swimming behind him, with her face down in the water,
she pulled two strokes and turned her face out to the side
for a breath and pulled one, methodically establishing her
rhythm. She felt her feet kick behind her. On each breath-
stroke she watched her right arm rise streaming from the
water as though it were lighter than air, and then her face was
back down in the warmth, and she was plowing two deep
furrows of tiny bubbles into the dark liquid beneath and
around her.

Then, after a while—she couldn't say just how she knew—
she felt that something was wrong. She stopped swimming

and looked across the water at J. T. His movements in the water must have attracted her attention.

What the hell?—was he drowning? No, that wasn't exactly it, though it might be. He seemed not to have gone under but to be stunned, floating vertically in the water. She couldn't tell. "Johnny," she called. Near him she saw for an instant a flick of black, like the tail of a deformed fish. J. T.'s short hair undulated against his neck.

"Johnny!" she called, more frantic now. "J. T.—what the fuck is going on?" Green-black water lapped softly into his mouth and out again. He did not answer. If this is a joke, you bastard . . . Probably it's just a joke.

She approached him from behind, cautious. She called out his name several times, but there was no response. When she was close enough, she reached over J. T.'s right shoulder and took his chin firmly in her hand.

As soon as she did, he sank like a stone. He had fainted. Dead weight.

Molly went under with him, tightening her grip on his chin. Through the sudden boil of bubbles she thought she saw the strange fish again, but before she could think of it she struggled her way back up to the surface and air. She felt J. T. stir slightly, she felt him float, perhaps instinctively, even in semi-consciousness.

"J. T.," she said. Her face was streaming with water. "Wake up." He was heavy and slick but not as hard to hold as he had first been or as she had imagined he would be. "You fainted," she said, and laughed, a little unexpectedly, hysterically, as she said it.

J. T. showed signs of waking up. Holding him became easier. With his chin still gripped in her hand, she used her forearm like a lever against his back. His legs floated up and he became easier to tow. She began her swim back to shore.

After a minute, she released his chin, careful not to drop him, and slid her arm across his chest and under his left arm. With difficulty she scissored her way through the water. The cross-chest carry was the closest they had come to an embrace. She couldn't avoid regretting the reversal of her old lifeguard fantasy. She should be the one drowning, not stuck with a dangerous rescue that she would probably fuck up.

She swam on. She was surprised at her own strength and presence of mind. She was intrigued by the feel of J. T.'s body. Even in her growing exhaustion she felt a momentary impulse to reach down and stroke his prick. As long as he was mostly unconscious anyway. She didn't do it. She couldn't. For one thing she would probably drop him and he would drown. "Yes, officer," she heard herself say to the investigating policeman, "I was towing him in by his penis and drowned him." It was something to think about, especially for a person having as much difficulty as Molly was beginning to have as she became more tired.

She stayed calm and swam steadily, holding him in the cross-chest position. She stretched out her long legs so that sometimes she could see her feet beneath the water.

Then she saw something else. The deformed fish. More clearly than ever.

Goodbye, J. T., she thought in terror, you'll just have to drown. But she didn't let go. The fish seemed to be about three feet long, trailing behind as though it were following them. She breathed deeply and swam on.

It was a lamprey, an eellike fish. She had seen them once before, with her father, when she was a child. Harmless, as far as she knew—she couldn't really remember.

Sometimes it was more clearly visible than other times, but it seemed to be swimming beneath her, or maybe between her and J. T. Or even, at times, between his legs.

Don't think about the eel, she thought, just don't think about it. Thank God she had not played with J. T.'s prick. She imagined herself reaching down for a feel and finding instead a three-foot living writhing monster with gills and pectoral fins. I will never go on another blind date. Not on any kind of date. Ever.

As she swam the eel swam too and seemed always to stay in about the same relationship to them. Once it lifted its spineless body into a strange loop so that its back showed for a moment above the surface of the lake like a sea monster, but in the air the lamprey was not so ugly. It was fawn-colored. It did not vary its path or change its position except slightly. Sometimes it floated closer to the surface, sometimes it seemed to have drifted a little to the right or left.

Very tired now, she looked at the shoreline to be certain she had not confused the time and distance. She had not.

Lampreys can attach themselves to other fish, she thought. That's what she had been trying to remember. It's how they eat. Couldn't they do it just as well to J. T.? Her father had showed her a trout with a half-dozen or so stuck to its sides, some no more than three inches long, trailing like banners. They slowly drained a fish's blood. Parasitic little sons-of-bitches. The sucker mouth draws the blood. She didn't know how long all this would take. Probably a long time. It could be hours, for all she knew. Days. It had to be, didn't it? She mustn't worry. J. T. must have seen the fish and stopped swimming, scared half to death probably. It could have attached itself if he were still for a second or two.

Then an even worse thought got in. Where it was attached. Could there be any doubt about it? It was on his prick, like an extension hose. The thought was staggering. How could a person stand it? How could J. T? No, hell no, she thought. It couldn't be there. He had on the swimsuit. Thank you Jesus for swimsuits. Yet somehow even knowing this, that it was a physical impossibility for the eel to be on his genitals, she didn't feel comforted.

Swimming on, more and more slowly because of her fatigue, she wondered how long they had before there was a danger, before it could actually bore in and start sucking blood. She was almost too tired to care. There was probably more likelihood they would drown first anyhow. All she could do was swim. If only there were some safe way to shift J. T. to the other arm. She didn't try.

The shore was extremely close now. She could see the spot in the woods where they had sat. And, unexpectedly, she could see Aunt Louise waving at them, far down the shoreline. They had told Aunt Louise where they would be, when Molly went to the house to change into her swimsuit. Now here she was. It was like a dream. Molly swam on.

Whenever the lamprey touched her leg Molly's sidestroke became frantic and clumsy, though now it touched her and she hardly noticed. She was less and less afraid. She was exhausted. Aunt Louise was walking along a path, still some distance away. She was carrying a silver cocktail shaker and glasses.

When Molly thought the water might be shallow enough to stand in, she pulled four more hard strokes, her arms burning, and stopped swimming. Her feet sank beneath her into the mud and she held onto J. T. Her breathing was heavy and ragged.

She looked for the fish, but saw nothing. J. T. was standing, almost by himself but leaning heavily upon her.

The two of them stood for a long time without moving. At last Molly could breathe more normally. She surprised herself by reaching into the water and feeling around for the lamprey.

As she groped between J. T.'s legs she spoke soothingly to him. When she had checked his crotch and the fish was not there, as she knew it could not have been, she felt better.

She kept searching. She ran her hand along J. T.'s legs, she reached as deeply into the water as she could. Nothing. What would she do if she found it?

Then, as she drew her hand back toward the surface, it thumped against the lamprey's strange body.

Her insides leaped. It was higher up than she had expected. She could see nothing, but the long eellike creature seemed to float horizontally at about waist level.

Reaching down, she found it again, and it moved at her touch. She put her hand around the fish and felt its body, muscular and firm. Though she could not hold it long before it squirmed from her grip, she was able to run her hand along its body, not even frightened now, until she found its head.

The sucker-disc mouth was stuck solidly to the skin of J. T.'s right side. For a few seconds she ran her fingers around the spot where J. T. and the lamprey were connected. She touched the little round lips, the size of a quarter, and she smoothed her hand along the body until the dorsal fin quivered beneath her touch.

J. T. was half-crying, paralyzed with fear.

"It's all right, John Thomas," she said. "You're fine. It's all right."

He was confused, distraught. She considered simply jerking the eel away from him if she could, but she hesitated. The spiny little teeth might already be boring in. She wanted to joke about it but could not.

"Snake," J. T. whispered, "snake . . ." J. T. was more awake now, he could stand by himself. His voice was a slow coarse whisper. "I've been bit by a snake."

"No, John Thomas, no," she said, like a mother. "It wasn't a snake. It was an eel—not even a real eel, a lamprey."

He didn't seem to hear.

With the lamprey trailing between them they walked a little toward shore into shallower water. J. T. stopped. "I can't go any more," he said.

"Take it easy, John, take it easy. Lampreys are harmless. Sort of. As soon as we get out of the water, we can pry it off, maybe. Or—or we can take you to a . . ." Who could help them?

His face became a death's head as she watched it. His eyes grew wide and vacant, his lips curled back. He had not known the fish was on him.

He ran for shore. He was not crying, not even screaming. He vomited sound.

Molly chased after him, she called out his name. She heard Aunt Louise cry out, for now she too had seen the fish. Molly saw only the frightened boy and the eel. Even in shallow water the eel hung on, and it still hung on when J. T. left the water altogether and ran aimlessly upon the lakebank. Finally his movements were a comic and terrible turning and half-turning as he stood in one spot. The lamprey clung to him, swinging this way and that, like the untied sash of a little girl's dress.

As Molly caught up with him she grabbed the lamprey and yanked. The mouth popped away from J. T.'s body with a swack. There was no blood.

J. T. sank to the ground with his face hidden between his knees. Molly stood and watched him and did not know what to say.

She carried the lamprey back to the water. For a moment the lamprey lay in the shallows above Molly's hand, then swam away.

Molly walked up the bank, more tired than she had ever

been. Aunt Louise was sitting near J. T. in the foreground of the ash-colored trees. She seemed uncertain, and was neither with J. T. nor away from him. Molly felt love for her aunt, and for the first time she felt sorry for her.

Molly wanted to help her, to make her know what had been going on, except that Molly was not sure herself. So much of what she had just done seemed unconnected with herself.

She walked over to the spot where she had left her shirt. Her arms and legs still ached from the swim, and now suddenly she was very sleepy.

The swimsuit was too much for her. She pulled down first the straps, then the whole top portion of the suit, so that her large breasts swung out free. She put on the shirt and buttoned it carefully. The bra portion of her suit flapped in front of her like an apron.

Molly lay down in the grass and felt the Gulf breeze push the grass against her skin.

Molly wondered whether anything ever really changes.

J. T. was crying softly and Molly loved him and hoped she had not embarrassed him by saving him. Aunt Louise moved close to Molly and took her hand into her own.

THE ATTENDANT

Winston pulled the stick and turned his wheelchair and motored out of the living room and negotiated the corners of the apartment and finally stopped in the bedroom near the bed. Harris followed close behind him. Harris was sixteen, and this was his first day on the job.

Harris pushed the hydraulic lift close to the wheelchair and fitted it in tight. He slipped a canvas strap beneath Winston's legs and another strap behind his shoulders and then he attached the straps by their metal hooks to the chains on the lift.

He pushed at the long handle on the lift until Winston began to rise up in the air. When Winston was a foot or two above the chair, dangling in the straps at the end of the chains and high enough to clear the bed, Harris heard him say, "At e-uf." It meant, "That's enough," and was the way Winston was forced to talk when he was bunched up into this odd bundle.

It was the first time Harris had seen Winston on the lift and he thought that Winston looked like a sack of grain, and this made his stomach feel a little queasy.

He concentrated on looking only at Winston's face, but this was not very pleasant either. Winston's eyes bulged and protruded from the pressure of hanging by the straps. Now Winston looked a little like a side of beef. The job was temporary, just until a permanent attendant could be found. Maybe it wouldn't take long to find somebody.

Harris positioned Winston above the bed and twisted the release valve slowly. The chains clanked and creaked and Winston was lowered, inch by inch, onto the sheepskin, first

his butt and then slowly backward. Harris put his hand behind Winston's head and neck as he would a baby and aimed
Winston at the pillow. Finally Winston was stretched out full
length on the bed.

Harris removed the straps and chains and pushed the lift
into a corner. All right, that wasn't so bad.

Harris began to undress Winston for bed. First the shoes,
then his socks and trousers and the support hose that kept
Winston's feet from turning blue, and then the shirt and the
corset.

Naked, Winston looked like a corpse. He was soft and white
and his arms and legs were atrophied and small. Harris suddenly believed they would never find a permanent attendant
to replace him.

Harris removed the leg-bag and pinched shut the opening
in the tube so the urine would not leak out. He held his breath
so that he did not smell the urine. He attached the catheter to
a tube that ran into a gallon milk jug beside the bed. It would
drain into the jug during the night and he would empty it in
the morning.

Taking care that he did not accidentally dump Winston off
the bed, Harris rolled him onto his right side and propped
him there with pillows behind his back. This would be Winston's sleeping position.

Winston's rear-end was flat as a squashed hat, from being sat
on all day. Harris could not even think about Winston's you-
know-what—his penis—which was the only normal-looking
part of him and so somehow the most abnormal part of all.
He flexed Winston's legs and separated his knees with a pillow
to prevent pressure sores. He put another pillow between
Winston's feet.

Now the worst part. After this it would be over. With a large
syringe, Harris drew irrigation fluid from a glass bottle and
forced the fluid, with slow pressure on the plunger, through
the catheter and into the stoma. He had looked at everything
but the stoma, and now he was having to look at it. It was a
strawberry-colored hole in Winston's lower belly, where the
catheter was permanently implanted, a place where the blad-

der had been pulled forward and turned back and surgically sewn onto the stomach. The fluid was dark yellow and thick and some of it bubbled up out of the hole in Winston's belly and had to be sopped up with gauze.

And so then that was that. The day was over. His first day on the job. He hated it and he hoped Winston would find a replacement for him right away and that he would never have to look at another sick or crippled person for the rest of his life, but the good part of it was that the day was over.

One of Winston's nightly medications was a sleeping pill, a strong sedative, so when Winston had swallowed that, it was not long before he was asleep.

Harris was tired. He went into his room, the room he would sleep in.

He undressed to his Jockey shorts and lay back on the bed. It was stuffy in the room, but he was too tired to try to open the window. He picked up a paperback novel he had brought with him and tried to read but he couldn't stay with it. He put the book aside.

He may have dozed for a while. When he looked at the clock, it was past midnight.

Harris was homesick. He thought of his mother putting up pints of dewberries at the kitchen sink, and of his father listening to old-fashioned music on the phonograph. He thought of his upstairs room—the only room he had ever had since he was a baby—with its deep angles in the ceiling and the luminous decals of stars and planets stuck to a portion of the ceiling over his bed.

He wished he knew someone to call. He realized for the first time how few friends he had. Even if it had not been past midnight he would not have known anyone to call.

He dialed a number for the time-of-day and listened to the friendly voice of the recording, a man, who spoke to him through the receiver. Next he called the weather and a recording of someone named Debbie started to talk to him.

Just then Harris heard Winston calling out from the other bedroom. Winston's voice was thick with the sleeping pill.

Harris hung up and went into Winston's room.

Winston said, "Did we remember the suppositories?"

Harris could tell what a great effort it took for Winston to come awake from the drugs and to deal with responsible matters.

Harris said, "Suppositories?—no, I don't think I knew about them."

Winston said, "And the chuck."

Now Harris remembered. Winston was supposed to have a bowel movement tonight. He had one once a week, and it just happened to fall on Harris' first day on the job. Harris knew of the procedure, he had just forgotten. Harris longed for his own bed and the tiny worlds on the ceiling above it.

Harris found the box of "chucks" in the supply closet— things that looked like huge paper diapers to be spread under Winston's hip to protect the sheepskin. And then the sup- positories, three of them. Harris felt a surge of panic overtake him for an instant, and then it subsided. He was not at all sure he could do this.

He held the three suppositories in his hand for a minute as if they were bullets. He stripped off the silver-colored foil and held them longer, looking at them in the half-light of the room. He opened the jar of Vaseline and greased them good, all three, and then, without any hope that he could look up a man's asshole and not be changed forever, he found the darkness at the center of Winston's flattened-out rear-end and stuffed in one suppository and then the second and then the final one and withdrew his hand, his index finger, and won- dered who on earth was this stranger occupying the same space as himself.

He washed his hands at the bathroom sink and floated— seemed to float!—to his bed and lay back on the sheets, mind- less and strangely happy, and did not even notice when he went to sleep.

At first Harris did not know what had waked him. He looked at his clock and saw that more than three hours had passed. He was groggy and confused. For a moment he believed he was at home—his parents' home—and that something was wrong, that someone was sick or in danger. Then he remembered that he was living with Winston.

Still he was not sure why he was awake. He considered this for a long time, two minutes maybe. As his head cleared, he understood that he had been wakened by a smell.

Harris struggled from his bed and bumped against a table and knocked something heavy onto the floor. It was the small suitcase he had brought with him. It contained all his clothes and his good shoes and a cap he never wore but that his mother had thrown in.

He groped his way over to the window and tried to open it and found that he didn't know how. He had lived in a house all his life, he didn't know how to open these dinky little apartment windows.

He had had no idea the smell was going to be so bad. He had not allowed himself to think of it at all. When he had greased and inserted the suppositories, he had allowed himself no fantasy of the results they might effect.

He wanted to hold onto something that he owned. He felt around in the dark for the suitcase. He picked it up and set it, at first, on the little table where it had been, and then on second thought put it on the bed where he had been sleeping. He felt along the wall for the light switch.

When the light was on he felt better. But the smell! The smell was like nothing else he had ever smelled before. No dog, no cat box, no baby's diaper, no open outhouse—nothing had ever smelled so bad as this.

He opened the door of his room. The smell buckled his knees. It was much worse in the hallway. His stomach heaved, but he forced it into submission.

He shut the door and turned off his light and hid in his dark room. He went back to his bed and lay down beside the suitcase. He held the suitcase to him like a lover, if he had ever held a lover. He broke into a sweat. His eyes were stinging. The smell was forever. It was as permanent as gravity, unavoidable.

He wanted to run away. It was not possible, he could not run.

He swung his legs off the bed. There was something new in him—like madness, and like prayer. He found the light switch, he opened his door again.

The smell was there, as fierce as an alligator, as fierce as grief.

He stepped into the hallway. He reeled around and bumped into the walls, he staggered and almost fell. It would get no worse than this.

And yet when he opened the door to Winston's room, it was much worse. A tomahawk of shit-smell struck him from ambush. Poisoned darts of shit-smell flew up his nose. He collapsed backward and caught himself in the doorframe.

This was a turning point, when he did not fall down and die. Suddenly he knew that he was invincible, he was superhuman. No power in heaven or on earth could fell him now. There was no such thing as unbearable sorrow, no pain that could not be borne. The world was a golden place, filled up with good souls and a loving God.

Harris turned on the light and saw that Winston was still sound asleep. The smell had not awakened him. The instinct to survive could wake a man from strong narcotics to ask for a laxative, but the smell of mere shit could not. It put life into perspective, it encouraged Harris and gave him hope for the future of man.

He looked down at the covers on Winston's bed, the massive corpse-like lump beneath them. The sheet and light blanket and spread would have to be pulled back.

He kept standing there. He didn't want to do it.

He remembered that he should have plugged in Winston's chair before he went to bed, to recharge the battery. He would do that now, before he forgot again. He picked up the heavy cord and the plug and stuck the large end into the wall sockete and the small yellow tips into the chair receptacle. He turned the dial on the charger to five hours. He took as long as he could, doing this, but then he had to face the covers again.

It had to be done. Harris walked around to the far side of the bed, behind Winston's back. He took the covers in his hand, making certain he had them all, sheet, blanket, spread. He hoped the chuck was secure.

He pulled the covers back and exposed Winston's rear-end. No smell could harm him now.

No smell—but the sight of it sent him reeling backward again. No cow in the pastures could have made a plop so large as the one Harris was looking at. In fact, it looked exactly like cow plop. Same size, same shape.

Harris' surging stomach settled back into place. He tried to remember the fresh clean fragrance of the pastures nearby, a smell of large slow animals and of hay and red clover and fresh water and saltlicks on the posts. He could not make the cow-smell come to him.

Winston woke up. His voice was thick with the sleeping pill. He grunted something that Harris could not understand. Harris was amazed that he could feel miserable and joyous at the same time. Harris said, "Time for a little clean-up." He would have described his own voice as chirpy.

Winston said, "That's the, ah, that's just what . . ." He was too sleepy to finish.

Harris took the nearer side of the chuck between his fingers and gave a slow even tug, just an inch or two, to see what would happen. The chuck was backed with blue plastic, which slipped evenly along the sheepskin and brought the pile with it.

Harris stopped. That's the way it worked, then. He would pull it out, very carefully. He would make sure he kept the sheepskin clean. He might have to get some toilet paper. Then he would roll up the whole package and get rid of it.

That's what he did. It took a little while, but it was no problem.

When he was done, he put on his jeans and walked out the door with the rolled-up chuck and went to the Dempster dumpster in the parking lot and tossed it in.

The night air was clean and lovely. The clouds were rolling, and sometimes the moon showed itself from behind them. The streets were wet beneath his bare feet, and the street-lights were reflected in pools of water left by a light rain. Harris felt wonderful and awake and alive.

He went back inside the apartment, which did not smell so

bad as before. Opening the doors had seemed to help. Harris'
stomach was still jumpy, but he was not sick. He got a basin
and filled it with warm water. He took a washcloth from the
bathroom.

Winston was awake enough to say, in a sleepy voice, "All
done?"

Harris said, "Just about got her whipped." Nothing chirpy
about that voice, nothing phony.

He squeezed warm water through the cloth and began to
bathe Winston's rear-end. He dried Winston with a fresh towel
and pulled the covers up so that Winston would not become
chilled.

Harris turned and looked at the window in Winston's room
and saw that it opened to the side. He flipped a small latch
and moved the glass to the left. It slid easily and let in the
smell of summer rain and new greenery.

"Okay, then," Harris said, with confidence. "We'll get a few
more hours' sleep."

Winston said, "Uh, better, ah, get a few . . ." He was asleep
before he could finish.

Harris walked to the bathroom. So this was the way it was
going to be. That was all right. He emptied the water from
the basin into the bathroom sink and washed his hands. He
went into his own room and opened the window easily. The
slow soaking rain, which had started again, made its small
sound in the parking lot.

Harris lay in his bed and listened. He breathed deeply and
thought he could smell the cows, dry and dusty in their barns
somewhere across the fields beyond the road, and he was certain he could smell wet clover and hay bales and melting saltlicks and wooden troughs filled with rainwater.

Harris made coffee the next morning, and soon Winston was
awake. From the kitchen window Harris could see the slow
movement of tree limbs and telephone wires in the breeze,
and he saw the ungraceful flight of a flock of blackbirds.

Harris gave Winston his morning bath, there in the bed. He
used the same basin as he had used the night before. Harris
could look at every part of Winston's body without fear, even

at Winston's normal-looking penis, which was erect this morning and stayed erect during much of the bath. Even it did not seem grotesque. Harris powdered Winston's feet and pulled on the support hose and hitched up the corset that corrected Winston's spinal curvature. He fitted the leg-bag onto Winston's thigh and attached the bag to the catheter. Next his trousers and shirt, and next the clumsy ride on the hydraulic lift and into the wheelchair. Harris brushed Winston's teeth and shaved him with an electric razor and combed his hair.

He went to the living room and put music on the phonograph and heard the hum of Winston's chair as it motored through the house toward the kitchen table.

Harris knew nothing about the music Winston listened to. He looked at the album covers and saw a picture of Louis Armstrong as a young man. Louis Armstrong was the only face he recognized among the photographs on the albums. There was a band called King-something and another called Kid-something else.

Harris said, "There was a red place on your balls this morning, when I bathed you."

Winston said, "Hm."

Harris, "It was like a stripe. A bright red stripe."

Winston said, "Remember you set me up straight in the chair yesterday, when I had slumped down? It must have pulled my pants up around my scrotum. It could have caused a lesion."

Harris knew this was dangerous. He was disappointed in himself.

Winston said, "No harm done. It happens sometimes."

Harris said, "I'll do better. I'll be more careful."

Harris poured coffee. The music was still playing. It was not Louis Armstrong, it was somebody else. He didn't know how to listen to the music.

Harris put a long plastic tube into Winston's coffee cup and guided the other end to Winston's mouth. He watched Winston drinking the coffee—his high forehead, his wiry black hair, his big handsome face. Harris squatted and unzipped the zipper on Winston's trouser leg and checked the bag and found that it was filling properly. He gave Winston his medication—this pill for muscle spasms, this capsule for something else, this for something else again.

He walked behind Winston to the refrigerator and saw the back of Winston's head. There at the crown was a bald spot. It was a large piece of scar tissue left over from an operation, or maybe many operations.

He asked Winston about the scar and Winston only said, "I had two holes drilled in my head."

Harris sat at the table across from Winston and said, "I like this music, I think."

Winston kept drinking his coffee through the tube and said nothing at all. This seemed very right to Harris. It was a quiet grown-up life, Harris thought.

Mornings Harris bathed and dressed Winston. He cooked the coffee and scrambled the eggs and spooned them into Winston's mouth. He took Winston to the office where Winston worked as a counselor.

And then Harris was alone at the apartment. It was early summer, so there was no school. Sometimes Harris' mother called to see if Harris was all right, to ask if he was eating any vegetables, and he was always happy to hear her voice.

Once he went over to his parents' home for a visit and found no one at home. He let himself in with a key his mother kept in the bird-feeder and went up to his old room. He saw the blue nylon satchel he kept his soccer equipment in and for some reason he laughed, a little sadly, when he saw it.

He took the family dog for a walk through the woods of a park near the house and he felt for the first time in his life that he had a past.

Back at the apartment he listened to music on Winston's phonograph. He tried a record by someone called Sidney Bechet and found that he could pick out the saxophone from the other instruments and was happy to learn from the album jacket that this was Bechet himself. He listened and thought he could pick out a couple of other instruments as well, but he was not sure.

He read on the dust cover of the album that Bechet's "vibrato" was particularly strong, and he felt stupid that he did not know the meaning of the word.

Grab your coat and get your hat . . . , the horns told him. Somehow the words of the song were in his head, though he could not remember ever having heard the song before. *Leave your worries on the doorstep* . . . Every note seemed to apply directly to himself. *Just direct your feet* . . . A saxophone solo came on. Now he understood vibrato. A trumpet took over the melody, pure against the throaty voice of the saxophone. And then a trombone. How did he recognize it? He had never heard a record so clearly before. This was what it meant to be grown-up.

He turned off the phonograph and sat in the fullness of the silence around him.

There was one more thing that happened.

It was near the end of summer. Harris had held the job nearly three months now. School would be starting soon, his senior year.

Harris' replacement had been found, the permanent attendant. He was a middle-aged man, very short, a midget almost. He wore a dapper moustache that, along with his rolled-down white socks and run-down shoes and polyester shirts, made him look all the more foolish. Robert Armstrong was the new man's name.

He had no experience, Robert Armstrong admitted, but he needed this job, he said, he really did, and he sure was willing to learn, he could learn almost anything if he was given half a chance.

Harris was secretly pleased at the pathetic figure Robert Armstrong cut.

And Robert was very clumsy, it turned out. His hands trembled as Harris showed him how to irrigate the catheter. He averted his eyes at the sight of the stoma. With Robert Armstrong at the controls of the hydraulic lift, Winston looked like a daring trapeze act in the circus. The first erection Robert saw on Winston sent him into a spasm of hysterical giggling.

He forgot to plug the chair into the battery charger and Winston had to creep around at the slowest speed all the next day.

In private Winston asked Harris to stay and help train Robert Armstrong. Winston said, "I'm not so sure about this guy."

Harris said, "He's all right. Give him some time. He'll be fine, just fine."

Harris agreed to stay a few days, a week maybe. Robert could have the bedroom, Harris didn't mind sleeping on the sofa, no problem.

It was late August. The summer heat rose from the asphalt outside in the parking lot. Winston kept the air conditioning on high, to prevent excessive sweating and irritation. In the pastures cattle stood knee-deep in the black ponds.

The day came when it was time for the suppositories.

Harris had not mentioned the procedure to Robert until now. He said, "The Vaseline is there, on the bedside table." He held out his hand and showed Robert the little bullet-shaped devices in his open palm. He felt cruel and powerful and complete.

Robert's moustache twitched, his eyes stared straight ahead. Written on his face was the question, How badly do I need this job?

Robert Armstrong extended his hand and took the suppositories from Harris. He held them there and stared at them. He said, as if to explain something to someone, maybe to himself, "I am a bachelor."

Harris had never tortured anyone before. There are so few persons vulnerable to torture. And yet that was not the reason. The reason was that he had been a child until now. Torture was an act of adulthood, the same as love. What he had shared with Winston was love. It was marriage. The incredible intimacy, the physicality and shared need. And now this, whatever it was, this power.

Robert Armstrong had broken into a smelly sweat.

Harris said, "Just put them in."

Robert uncapped the jar of Vaseline. He dug in his index finger and brought out a glob of grease.

For a moment Harris was disappointed. He thought Robert had fully recovered himself. Robert's hand did not tremble. In his own prissy clumsy way Robert Armstrong seemed to be taking care of business.

Then Harris noticed that Robert was greasing the suppositories without having removed the foil wrappers.

Harris feigned gentleness and took the suppositories from Robert and removed the foil and showed him the correct procedure.

Winston was already drugged and lay snoring in the bed.

Harris pulled back the sheet and exposed Winston's rear-end. "Right there," Harris said, pointing.

Harris watched Robert Armstrong move into position and find the dark little puckered opening into Winston's squashed-hat ass, and then he watched the little bullets disappear, one two three, and he heard Robert Armstrong release a long sigh and withdraw his finger.

Waking on time was second nature to Harris now. He came awake on the sofa where he had slept these five days. There was a streetlight in the parking lot outside, the objects in the room seemed silvery and familiar.

He looked at the clock, and saw that a few hours had passed. He sat up and rubbed his face in his hands.

It was odd that he didn't smell anything. Was Winston slow tonight?

He walked to Winston's room and opened the door, and still there was no smell.

When he pulled back the covers there was nothing on the chuck.

He looked at the clock again. It should have happened by now.

He went back to the living room and lay on the sofa again and propped his head on his pillow and he thought, "I won't be able to go back to sleep," but the next thing he knew he was dreaming about trying to dial a telephone number and not being able to get it right.

He woke up and looked at the clock and saw that another

hour had passed. When he pulled back Winston's covers he saw that there was still nothing to clean up.

In a couple more hours it would be daylight. This had never happened before.

Winston was awake now. He said, "What's going on?" in a voice not so sleepy as Harris might have expected.

Harris said, "Nothing's happening."

Winston said, "I thought so."

Harris said, "How did you know?"

Winston said, "My face. The tingling in my face is so fierce, it's like somebody jangling bells."

Harris said, "We'll try again later."

Winston said, "It has to be done now."

Harris said, "What has to be done?"

At this moment Robert Armstrong came into the room, tiny and sleepy and confused. Robert said, "Is everything all right?" He looked like one of the seven dwarves in his long sleepshirt and cracked leather bedroom slippers.

Winston's voice was strong, even above the drugs. He said, "There's a bit of a dangerous situation. Harris has it under control."

Harris said, "Danger?"

Winston said, "It will have to be dug out."

Harris said, "Dug out?"

Winston said, "With your fingers."

Many years later Harris would remember this failure of his nerve and would wonder what it had to do with the course of his life, his failures and his new starts and his letting go of regret.

That night there was no question: Harris could not do what had to be done.

Harris wondered whether Robert Armstrong saw this night through the same unhappy silvery haze that he himself watched through.

He saw Robert Armstrong move into position behind Winston. He saw Robert's hand disappear inside of Winston.

And when he saw Robert draw forth the first of the nine or

ten nuggets that he would produce from this strange familiar mine of a body, this physical warmth to which Harris had felt married and which he now believed he had betrayed, he watched Robert Armstrong hold out his hand with the first hard brown walnut-sized object in it.

What did Robert mean, holding it there? It was not triumph, not worship, not fear.

Robert said nothing. Harris said nothing.

For an instant Harris believed Robert was handing the nugget to him, and for the briefest second he considered taking it.

Instead Robert placed it on the chuck and again reached his hand inside Winston's body and brought out a second one like the first and lay it on the chuck also and went back again and again and again until it was finished.

Harris watched him and expected him to change miraculously, to become a confident swaggering pirate, at least to grow taller. Nothing of the kind happened.

It surprised Harris when Robert spoke. Robert said, "My mother stays up half the night watching programs."

Harris said, "I'll be moving back with my parents in the morning."

Robert carefully wadded up the chuck and lay it aside and covered Winston's rear-end.

Harris said, "Sometimes I listen to Winston's music."

Robert said, "It happens over and over. There are too many new lifetimes to count."

THE ALL-GIRL
FOOTBALL TEAM

Dressing in drag was not new to me. I had never worn a dress myself, but my father had.

My father was all man. His maleness defined him to me. Evenings, when he came home from work, I loved to hug him and to feel the rasp of a day's growth of beard against my face and neck. I loved to smell him, a fragrance of wool and leather and whiskey and shoepolish and aftershave.

Drag was not a frequent thing, only twice a year. Halloween, of course. Kids in costume would come to our house and ring the bell and Father would answer it in women's clothes. "Trick or treat, Gilbert," the children would say, and my father would try to guess who was behind each mask. He would drop candy into the plastic pumpkins or paper sacks and send the children on to the next house.

The other time was the Womanless Wedding. It was an annual affair, a minstrel show in rouge instead of blackface. The Rotary and the Lions—all the solid male citizens of Arrow Catcher, Mississippi—would put on a raucous play in drag and donate the money to charity. One year Mr. Rant got drunk and fell off the stage in a floor-length gown.

My father loved the Womanless Wedding. He took a different part each year: bride, mother of the bride, flower girl, maid of honor, whatever was available. He shaved his legs and Naired his chest and bleached the hair on his arms and plucked his eyebrows and rouged his lips and mascaraed his lashes and he was ready. He owned wigs. With a pedicure and a close shave, my father was a pretty good looking woman for his age.

So dressing in drag was not new.

In my junior year of high school, my class got the idea of putting on an all-girl football game. We were raising money for some worthwhile project or other—a new scoreboard for the gym, I think. The idea was for the junior and senior girls to put on uniforms and helmets and to play football against each other. The school principal agreed to let us use the stadium. We would charge admission and sell hot dogs and Cokes at the concession stand.

It seemed like a good idea.

The idea seemed even better when I first saw the girls in uniform. They were beautiful. Hulda Raby had long legs and boyish hips and large breasts, and when she was dressed in our school colors and was wearing pads and cleats and a rubber mouthpiece, I thought no one on earth had ever had such a good idea as the all-girl football team.

The girls were enthusiastic. They found a senior boy who agreed to coach them, Tony Pirelli, whose father owned the Arrow Cafe.

Positions were tried out for and assigned. Plays were drawn up and mimeographed and passed out to the players and carried around in notebooks and memorized. A wide-hipped girl named Tootie Nell Hightower learned to snap the ball, and Nadine Johnson learned to take the snap from center.

I stood on the sidelines and watched Nadine hunker into position behind the center's upturned rear-end and put her hands into position. *Green forty-two* . . . My heart jumped out of my chest.

Pads began to clash, helmets to clatter. Nadine was a natural at quarterback and could throw the bomb. Ednita Gillespie could get open. I saw these girls through new eyes. I feared them and I loved them.

The days passed. No one except the players was allowed inside the locker room, of course, not even Tony Pirelli, the kid who coached them. But each day after practice I hung outside in the parking lot and imagined them in there. I saw them unlace their cleats and fling them into a corner. I saw them strip dirty tape from their ankles and remove the Tuff-skin with alcohol. I smelled the pungency of their skin. I watched them walk through the locker room wearing only their shoulder-pads, nothing else, the padding stained with sweat. I watched them soap up in the shower and play grabass and snap each other with towels. I saw them stand under the shower and let the water pour into their upturned faces and I watched one or another of them relax her bladder and allow the urine to run down her leg and swirl away in the drain.

Never before in the history of the whole wide world had anyone ever had such a good idea as the all-girl football team.

I wanted to be near the girls. I hung around the parking lot to watch them. At first a few other boys did the same, and we punched each other's arms and made jokes, but my interest outlasted theirs and soon I was the only boy in the parking lot.

My favorite part of the day was when the girls came out of the locker rooms after practice, after their showers.

Nadine Johnson came out, the quarterback. She had short hair and it was still wet and slicked back like a man's. Hulda Raby had blonde hair that hung down to her hips. One day she stepped out of the gym into the late afternoon sun and bent over and allowed her wet hair to hang down over her face, almost to the ground. She toweled it roughly with a white locker room towel and then flung her hair back over her head so that it hung down her back again. She dropped the towel behind her, arrogant, and she seemed to know that someone would pick it up for her. It was my joy to rush across the lot and place the towel into a bin of soiled linens.

Hulda Raby did not notice me, of course. My reward was to be close to the locker room door when the others came out.

Tootie Nell Hightower, the center—I could not look at her without seeing her bent over the ball, its leather nap gripped in her certain hands. Lynn Koontz—I heard the beauty of her name for the first time. It was a football player's name. You could play tight end for the Steelers with a name like Lynn Koontz. The twins, Exie Lee and Nora Lee Prestridge. The Sewell girls, Marty and Ruby. Ednita Gillespie, the wide receiver. I heard Nadine say to her, "Nita, honey, you got a great pair of hands."

I envied them their womanhood.

I watched them on the practice field each day after school. Tony Pirelli, their coach, seemed to me the luckiest boy in the world.

I insinuated myself into their midst. I volunteered to act as a flunky for the team. I helped line the field. I asked parents to act as referees and scorekeepers, and I made sure everyone had clean socks. I carried equipment and water bottles and the first aid kit. I saddlesoaped footballs and replaced broken elastic. I dealt with the high school principal, who was worried about the light bill, since the game was to be held at night.

It was springtime and the Mississippi Delta was Eden to me. I saw it as I had never seen it before, the whippoorwills and coons and owls and little bobwhites. Mornings the pecan trees outside my window were heavy with dew and smelled like big wet flowers.

In my dreams I listened to the music of *green forty-two hut hut hut* . . . It floated on the air like a fragrance of wisteria. I knew why men married, as my father had, and were true to the same woman over a lifetime. I thought of my father's mortality.

I went into my father's room and found his revolver and broke it open and poured its cartridges onto the chenille bedspread. I thought of my own mortality. I understood for the first time the difficulty of ever knowing who I am. I longed to be held as a lover by a woman in a football suit.

The all-girl football team idea got out of hand. It became elaborate.

Somebody suggested that we should have boy cheerleaders, dressed up in girls' cheerleading costumes. It would be hilarious, everybody said. What fun. Somebody else thought it would be just great if we made it homecoming as well. You know, with a homecoming court. Everyone agreed, Sure! Oh boy! It would be like the Womanless Wedding, only better. We'll hold the ceremony at halftime. We'll crown a homecoming queen!

I didn't like the idea. I said, "I'm against it. It's a silly idea. I vote no."

Everybody else said, "It'll be hilarious. Let's do it, sure it's great."

I wanted to say, Are you insane? We have discovered what makes women beautiful. The girl-children who were our classmates three weeks ago are now women—they are constellations! Do you want a constellation walking in a parade with some goon in a dress?

Instead I said, "No way. I'm not doing it. I've got to line the field. I've got to pump up the balls. Count me out, brother."

I did it anyway. I was elected cheerleader. That's small-town high school for you. It was a big joke. I didn't want to do it, so everybody voted on me. No try-outs, nothing. One day I get the news and a box with a cheerleader costume in it. I said, "Forget it."

Everybody said, "Be a sport."

Right up until the night of the big game I still wasn't going to do it. I wasn't even going to the game. Why should I? Nobody was taking the game seriously—nobody but me and the girls who were knocking their heads together.

Maybe this will explain it: One day after practice I saw Ednita Gillespie get into her father's pickup alone. She yanked open the door and, as she did, she put her fingers to one side of her nose and blew snot into the gravel driveway of the schoolhouse parking lot. The door banged shut behind her and she drove away.

Do you understand what I mean? It was not Ednita I loved. Not Tootie Nell or Lynn Koontz or Nadine Johnson. It was Woman. I had never known her before. She was a presence as essential and dangerous as geology. Somehow she held the magic that could make me whole and give me life.

That's why I wasn't going to the all-girl football game.

I said all this to my father in his room at the back of our house. In this room I could say anything. I could smell my father's whole life in this room, the guns in the closet, the feathers of birds he had killed, the blood of mammals, the mutton that greased the line of his fly-casting equipment.

I said, "It would take a fool. To dress up like a girl, when there are women—women, Daddy, not girls—dressed in pads and cleats."

What do you suppose my father said to me? Can you guess? Do you think he said, "Don't be silly, it's a school project. I want you to participate." Do you think he said, "It's up to you, of course, but I just want to tell you, you're going to be missing out on a whole lot of fun."

My father was a housepainter. He went to sixth grade and no further. He said, "I will dress you in a skirt and a sweater and nice underwear and you will feel beautiful."

I said, "Uh . . ."

He said, "You have never felt beautiful."

I said, "Well . . ."

It was near dark. The fall air had turned cold. In two hours the all-girl football game would begin. My mother was still at work.

Father drew my bath and put almond oil into the water and swished the water back and forth with his hand until it foamed up. He hung a green silk bathrobe on a hook on the bathroom door. He set out bathpowder and a powder puff he had bought new for me. He showed me how to shave my legs and underarms. It didn't matter that no one else would be able to see.

When I was clean and sweet-smelling, I came into his room wearing the robe. He gave me the clothes I would dress in.

I said, "Dad, is this queer?"

He did not answer.

I took the box with the uniform in it, and a small bag with new underwear.

I slipped into the lacy underpants, and then into the panty-hose.

I let him show me how to hook the bra, which he did not stuff with Kleenex. He gave me tiny false breasts, cups made of foam rubber, with perfect nipples on the ends. When I slipped on my sweater with the big AC on the front, you could see my nipples showing through.

I put on a half-slip and the skirt. He showed me how to apply my makeup. I could choose any wig I wanted. He spritzed me with Windsong.

I did not feel beautiful. I felt like a fool. I looked at myself in the mirror and saw that I looked like a fool as well. I stood like a boy, I walked like a boy, I scratched myself like a boy. I had a dumb boy-look on my face. My hands were boy-hands. My dick, for no good reason, was stiff and aching.

The masculine smells of my father's room—the rubber raingear and gun oil and fish scales stuck to his tacklebox— reached me through my false femininity and mocked me.

My father said, "How do you feel?"

I said, "Like a fucking fool."

I said, "I've got a hard on."

He said, "Do you know any cheers? Can you do one cheer for me before you go?"

I said, "I don't think so, Dad."

He said, "Well, I'll have my eyes on you the whole game. I'll be watching you from the stadium."

I said, "I wish there was a Book of Life, with all the right answers in the back."

He said, "Do 'Satisfied.' Just once, before you go. 'Satisfied' is my favorite cheer."

There was something about that football field: the brilliant natural carpet of green grass, the incredible lights, the strong straight lines of chalkdust, the serviceable steel bleachers filled with cheering people and the little Arrow Catcher High School marching band in uniform—there was something in all that scene that told me who I was. I did not feel beautiful, as my father had predicted. I was the same person I had always been, and yet the bass drum, with its flaking bow-and-arrow design and the words ARROW CATCHER, MISSISSIPPI, printed in faded letters around the perimeter of the drum-head, told me that the worst things about myself were not my enemies and that the Womanless Wedding held meaning for my father that I might never understand and did not need to understand.

I had come to the game late. The referees in their striped

suits had already taken the field. The opposing teams, in black and gold uniforms, had finished warm-up calisthenics. Steel whistles sounded and drew the players from their final huddle and prayers.

The captains walked like warriors to the middle of the field. They watched the toss of the coin.

I watched it also, from the sidelines. The coin went up and up. It seemed suspended in the air beneath those blazing lights, above the green table of Delta land. The coin seemed forged of pure silver and big as a discus. It turned over and over, as if in slow motion. It hung for a century.

I jumped up and down in my wool skirt and saddle oxfords. I was a cheerleader at the center of the universe. I waved my pom-poms and clapped my hands and kicked my heels up behind me. I tossed my hair and fluttered my lashes without knowing I knew how to do these things. The coin that I was watching was a message of hope and goodness throughout the land.

It was a land I loved, this fine ellipse in a crook of the Yazoo River—its alligators and mallards and beaver dams, its rice paddies and soybeans and catfish farms.

Suddenly I knew that my father was right, that I did feel beautiful, except that now beauty had a different meaning for me. It meant that I was who I was, the core of me, the perfect center, and that the world was who it was and that those two facts were unchangeable. Grief had no sting, the future was not a thing to fear, all things were possible and personal and pure.

I watched the opening kickoff. It was a short grounder that scooted between the legs of the front line of girls in uniform.

By the time someone in the backfield picked it up, my small breasts had become a part of me, not rubber but flesh. My cock, beneath the lacy underpants, was what it had always been, this odd hard unpredictable equipment I had been born with, and yet it was also a moist opening into the hidden fragrance of another self that was me as well. My arms were woman-arms, my feet woman-feet, my voice, my lips, my fingers. I stood on the sweet sad brink of womanhood, and somehow I shared this newness with my father.

The game had begun, and I was the cheeriest cheerleader on the sidelines. One team scored a touchdown. Hulda Raby sustained a serious knee injury. Nadine threw the bomb to Ednita but had it intercepted. The band played the fight song, and we went through all the cheers.

My father and mother were in the bleachers, far up, and I could see the pride in their faces. I was a wonderful cheerleader, and they knew that I was.

We did "Satisfied," and in my heart I dedicated the cheer to my father.

I went to the principal, we cheerleaders called out, with our hands on our hips, sashaying as we pretended to walk haughtily into the principal's office.

Satisfied, came the refrain back from the cheering section, including my father and mother.

And the principal said, we called out, shaking our finger, as if the principal were giving us a stern talking-to.

And again the loud refrain, *Satisfied.*

That we couldn't lose . . .

Satisfied . . .

With the stuff we use . . .

Satisfied . . .

You take-a one step back . . . Here we put our hands behind our backs and jumped one step backward, cute and coy, as if we were obeying the principal's stern order.

Satisfied . . .

You take-a two steps up . . . Here we put on a look of mock surprise, as if we just could not understand what the principal was getting at with all his complicated instructions, but we put our hands on our hips and took two cute steps forward anyway.

The principal's final line is: *And then you strut your stuff, And then you strut your stuff, And then you strut your stuff.* Which we did, by wagging our sexy hips and prankishly twirling our index fingers in the air.

Sat-isss-fied!

The Mississippi Delta air was the Garden of Eden, filled with innocence and ripe apples. The blue of the skies shone through the darkness of the night and through the glare of

the stadium lights. I smelled fig trees and a fragrance of wee-
vil poison and sweet fishy water from the swamp.

The game went on. The huddles and the time-outs, the sweat
and the bloody noses and the fourth-down punts.

And then halftime. I had literally forgotten all about halftime.

My whole world exploded into ceremony and beautiful rit-
ual. The band was on the field in full uniform. The goalposts
were wrapped in black and gold crepe paper, and streamers
were blowing in the autumn breeze. Boys with shaven legs
strutted past the bleachers wearing majorette costumes. They
carried bright banners on long poles. The band marched in
formation, and then it formed a huge heart in the center of
the field. It played "Let Me Call You Sweetheart," and I felt
tears of joy and the fullness of nature well up in me. I knew
that the world was a place of safety and hope and that my father was a great man. I knew that I was a beautiful woman
and that because of this I had a chance of growing up to be as
fine a man as my father. *Let me call you sweetheart I'm in love with
you, Let me hear you whisper that you love me too.* I loved the girls
in uniform; I would always love them. They were lined up
under the home-team goalposts with the maids of the homecoming court. *Keep the lovelight burning in your eyes so true . . .*
Nadine Johnson was the captain. She led the beautiful slow
processional of players and maids toward the center of the
field. The band played. There was a sweetness of Mowdown
in the air from the rice paddies nearby.

I knew the meaning of love. I thought of my father, the way
he had looked on the day of his wedding, the first of his wed-
dings that I was old enough to attend. He had been the bride
and had worn a high-bodice floor-length gown, antique white,
with a train and veil. He carried a nosegay at his waist. When
the minister asked whether any person here present could
show just cause why this couple should not be joined in holy
matrimony, a drunken pharmacist named H. L. Berryman,
wearing a print dress and heels, jumped up out of the audience and fired a pistol in the air. My father fell into a swoon.

It was all part of the show, of course—and although I knew

it was only a play and that my father was only an actor in it, I wanted to leap from my seat in the audience and make known to all the world that he was my father and that without him my own life was without meaning.

On the football field Nadine Johnson turned to a tiny boy-child, three or four years old, who was a part of the homecoming ceremonies. He was wearing a ruffled dress with stiff petticoats and was standing beside Nadine with a satin pillow in his hands. There was a silvery crown on the pillow. The homecoming court was assembled around them, arms hooked in arms, smiles bright.

Nadine took the crown from the pillow, as flashbulbs went off.

A boy named Jeep Bennett was standing beside Nadine. He was wearing a yellow evening gown and had only three fingers on one hand. He had been in a hunting accident the year before and this year had been elected homecoming queen.

Nadine placed the crown on his proud head, and the flashbulbs went off again. The bleachers roared with applause and cheers and approval. Nadine kissed Jeep, and Jeep was demure and embarrassed.

I had wanted—dreamed!—of this moment, dreaded it in a way, because I had believed I would envy Jeep this perfection, this public kiss of a woman in a football suit, which I had believed for three weeks was the completion of love and sex and holy need.

And yet now that it was here, it was oddly meaningless to me. There was no jealousy in my heart, no lust for Nadine in all her sweaty beauty.

And yet there was lust in my heart, sweet romance. My breath caught in my throat, my tiny breasts rose and my nipples hardened. (Seemed to harden, I swear!)

I looked down the line of suited-up women and their male maids. Tootie Nell, wide-hipped and solid; Hulda, with a damaged knee; Lynn Koontz, her magical name. I looked at the drag-dressed boys who clung violet-like to the certain arms of these beautiful women.

And yes there was lust and even love in my heart, but not for the women in black-and-gold. The person I loved was

wearing a business suit with a back-pleat in the skirt, so that
when he walked you could see a triangle of his gray satin slip
and the back of his beautiful knee. Tony Pirelli, the kid who
coached the team, was an Italian boy with dark skin and dark
eyes and a nut-brown wig that caressed his shoulders. He
wore a soft gray silk blouse with ruffled sleeves and, at his
throat, a ruffled ascot. His shoes were patent leather sling-
back pumps with two-inch heels, and the girls had given him a
corsage, which he wore on his breast.

I hated my thoughts and my feelings. I was certain my father could read them all the way to the top of the bleachers.

I had never seen anyone so beautiful as Tony Pirelli. He
never smiled, and now his sadness called out to me, it made
me want to hold him and protect him from all harm, to kiss
his lips and neck, to close his brown eyes with my kisses, to
hold his small breasts in my hands and to have him touch my
own breasts.

I believed I was a lesbian. What else could I call myself? I
felt like a fool for not having noticed before. I was a fool for
having strutted my stuff during the cheers, for having loved
the Mississippi Delta and the sentimental songs played by the
band.

I didn't see the rest of the game. The band played and the
crepe paper rattled and the banners whipped and the crowds
cheered, and I ran away from the sidelines and through the
gate and away from the football field and the school grounds.

This happened in the autumn I was sixteen years old. Now I
am forty-five years old, and all of it seems too fantastic to be
true. Maybe my memory has exaggerated the facts, somehow.

I remember what happened afterward very accurately,
though.

I ran through the little town of Arrow Catcher, Mississippi,
toward my parents' home. I don't know what I wanted there,
the safety of my father's room, I think, the fishing rods and
reels with names like Shakespeare and Garcia, the suits of
camouflage and the rubber hip-waders. I was still wearing my
cheerleader costume and my makeup and false breasts and
even the wig.

And then something happened, by magic I suppose, that stopped me. The Southern sky seemed to fill with light—no, not light, but with something like light, with meaning, I want to say.

I stood in the street where I had stopped and I listened to the distant brass of the Arrow Catcher High School marching band. It sounded like the blare of circus horns. I took deep breaths and exhaled them into the frosty air.

I took from my skirt pocket the lace handkerchief my father had put there for me, and I dabbed at my eyes, careful not to smear the mascara more than it was already smeared.

I began walking back toward the football field. I was not a woman. I did not feel like a woman. I was not in love with a boy. I was a boy in costume for one night of the year, and I was my father's child and the child of this strange southern geography. I was beautiful, and also wise and sad and somehow doomed with joy.

The gymnasium was decorated in black and gold. There was a table with a big crystal punch bowl, and other tables with ironed white tablecloths and trays of sandwiches and cookies. Around the walls of the gym our parents had placed potted plants and baskets of flowers. The girls had changed to their party dresses, the boys had put on the trousers and sport jackets our parents had brought for us. We were proper boys and girls, and our costumes were stuffed into bags in the locker rooms where we changed.

A phonograph blared out the music we loved.

I danced close to Nadine Johnson and imagined, as I felt her cool cheek against mine, that I could see the future. I imagined I would marry—not Nadine but some woman like Nadine, some beautiful woman, faceless for now—and that together we would have sons and that we would love them and teach them to be gentle and to love the music we were dancing to and to wear dresses and that, in doing this, we would somehow never grow old and that love would last forever.

ABOUT THE AUTHOR

Lewis Nordan, a native of Itta Bena, Mississippi, is assistant professor of creative writing at the University of Pittsburgh. His stories have appeared in the *Greensboro Review, Harper's, Redbook,* and the *Southern Review.*

VINTAGE
CONTEMPORARIES

84/4.3

V I N T A G E
CONTEMPORARIES

___ **Soft Water** by Robert Olmstead	$6.95	394-75752-1
___ **Family Resemblances** by Lowry Pei	$6.95	394-75528-6
___ **Norwood** by Charles Portis	$5.95	394-72931-5
___ **Clea & Zeus Divorce** by Emily Prager	$6.95	394-75591-X
___ **A Visit From the Footbinder** by Emily Prager	$6.95	394-75592-8
___ **Mohawk** by Richard Russo	$6.95	394-74409-8
___ **Anywhere But Here** by Mona Simpson	$6.95	394-75559-6
___ **Carnival for the Gods** by Gladys Swan	$6.95	394-74330-X
___ **Myra Breckinridge and Myron** by Gore Vidal	$8.95	394-75444-1
___ **The Car Thief** by Theodore Weesner	$6.95	394-74097-1
___ **Breaking and Entering** by Joy Williams	$6.95	394-75773-4
___ **Taking Care** by Joy Williams	$5.95	394-72912-9

On sale at bookstores everywhere, but if otherwise unavailable, may be ordered from us. You can use this coupon, or phone (800) 638-6460.

Please send me the Vintage Contemporaries books I have checked on the reverse. I am enclosing $_____ (add $1.00 per copy to cover postage and handling). Send check or money order—no cash or CODs, please. Prices are subject to change without notice.

NAME _____

ADDRESS _____

CITY _____ STATE _____ ZIP _____

Send coupons to:
RANDOM HOUSE, INC., 400 Hahn Road, Westminster, MD 21157
ATTN: ORDER ENTRY DEPARTMENT
Allow at least 4 weeks for delivery.

005   38